REVELATION REVEALED:

A Modern Interpretation

Wayne Hill
with our Lord Christ Jesus

CONTENTS

Introduction

Let us begin with what the book "Revelation Revealed: A Modern Interpretation" is really about. The Book of Revelation is not what we have learned in the past. First of all, "Revelation Revealed: A Modern Interpretation" is not going to try to interpret the symbolism in the Book of Revelation since, frankly, it can be interpreted in perhaps thousands of different ways. The reason the symbolism contained in the Book of Revelation cannot be interpreted is due to the fact it was never meant to be interpreted and I will explain later what I mean by that statement. Instead, it was meant to confuse and confound the reader and make our Lord God look like an evil deity. It is also a book of the holy Scriptures which was corrupted by Satanic influences. You will read a lot of evil in the Book of Revelation. If you have read Revelation you probably remember there are many number 7s in the Book of Revelation. The number 7 in the Book of Revelation represents Satan and is an evil number when viewed in the context of the Book of Revelation. Examples of holy numbers are 3, 6, 9, and 12. Sometimes '1' is considered a holy number as well. And, since there are so many instances of the number 7 in the Book of Revelation we then must conclude that Revelation is not going to reveal all truth. In fact, it was Satan's hope the Book of Revelation would so confuse those who read it they would then have doubts about our Lord God's love for His children. As you read the Book of Revelation you will see that, supposedly, there are angelic beings from heaven who do much of the destruction which leads to great death, hardship, and suffering on Earth. Can you imagine our Father using innocent angels in heaven who know nothing of evil to slaughter millions of people on Earth, including unborn babies, new born babies, toddlers, and small to not so small children? Could you imagine a Lord God who would do such a thing? The reason Satan corrupted the Book of Revelation is due to the fact it was Satan's hope to cause all of humanity to believe the Lord God was behind all the death, destruction, and misery on Earth instead of him. Our Lord Christ Jesus explained to us in the holy Scriptures that Satan is the ruler of this world.

Satan is the Ruler of this World

John 12:31
"The time for judging this world has come, when Satan, the ruler of this world, will be cast out"(NLT).

And Paul, writing in the book of 2nd Corinthians concurred with our Lord Christ Jesus with these words.

2nd Corinthians 4:4
"Satan, who is the god of this world, has blinded the minds of those who do not believe"(NLT).

This last verse tells us that Satan has the power to blind the minds of people who are not believers in order to keep them from ever knowing our Lord Christ Jesus. So, we should not be so quick to believe the Lord God is behind all of the horrible events which inflict this world. It has become such a strong belief in the Lord God controlling all events on Earth, including our lives, when catastrophe does strike it is often said, "it was an act of God." How Satan became the ruler of this world will be explained later in chapter 12.

According to what we read in the Book of Revelation the end-of-times is going to be the cause of literally billions of human deaths the world over. And, yet, we are told by our Lord Christ Jesus that our Father loves us more than we can love our own children, so how can this be? From the beginning of our reading of the Old Testament we are shown a "supposedly" loving Lord God torturing His own children and frightening many to death. In the Book of John our Lord Christ Jesus, while speaking with a few Pharisees, had this to say to them.

John 8:44-47

"For you are the children of your father the devil, and you love to do the evil things he does. He was a murderer from the beginning. He has always hated the truth, because there is no truth in him. When he lies, it is consistent with his character; for he is a liar and the father of lies. So when I tell the truth, you just naturally don't believe me! Which of you can truthfully accuse me of sin? And since I am telling you the truth, why don't you believe me? Anyone who belongs to God listens gladly to the words of God. But you don't listen because you don't belong to God"(NLT).

Also, in the Book of John our Lord Christ Jesus said this to the Pharisees present.

John 8:54

"You say, 'He is our God,' but you don't even know him'"(NLT).

The above holy Scripture reveals why we should take a second look at the Book of Revelation and realize it is not our Father in heaven who is orchestrating this worldwide suffering in its pages. Instead, it is Satan himself. Satan has long attempted to portray our loving, compassionate, kind, considerate, merciful, patient, forgiving, just, and wise Lord God as a vengeful, hateful, and jealous God. Christ Jesus speaks to us of a far different Lord God, one that is not vengeful, or hateful, or jealous; but, instead a very humble and caring God. In fact, one of the reasons our Lord Christ Jesus came to Earth to begin with was to reveal our Father in heaven to us.

Our Father in Heaven Loves Us Very Much

I am the way, the truth, and the life, says our Lord Christ Jesus. Not only was our Lord Christ Jesus the Son of the living Lord God, he was also an instrument of our Father in heaven who spoke through him and told him what to say. Christ Jesus often spoke of how he was saying what his Father told him to say and how to say it. Who else could make such a claim except one who knew our Father in heaven was using him to deliver a message to his children on Earth to love one another as He loves us. One day our Lord Christ Jesus was heard saying he was one with the Father and the Father was one with him. Meaning, they were one and the same. Our Lord Christ Jesus was always delivering a message of hope and never once did he tell his followers and those listening to him speak, that he was our Lord God. No, he never once did. He was a humble man who had been chosen by our Lord God to come to Earth to deliver a very important message, and that message was that our Father in heaven loves us so very much and we should love one another as our Father in heaven loves us.

The following quote is from the Book of John and it reads as follows.

John 12:49-50

"I don't speak on my own authority. The Father who sent me has commanded me what to say and how to say it. And I know his commands lead to eternal life, so I say whatever the Father tells me to say"(NLT).

Does this not answer the question of whether our Lord Christ Jesus came to reveal our Father to us? It says very clearly that our Father in heaven was speaking and working His miracles on Earth through our Lord Christ Jesus. Our Father was performing miracles and blessing people's lives and letting them know they were loved deeply by their Father in heaven through our Lord Christ Jesus. The Lord God chose to come to us directly through our Lord Christ Jesus to plead with us personally to love one another as He loves us. Does that sound like a Lord God who would destroy the children He loves so deeply?

Also, does this not prove the Lord God of the Old Testament is not always the Lord God of the New Testament? How could our Lord God love the Jews very deeply one day and the next day have them slaughtered by their enemies just to exact revenge or to discipline them for doing wrong? Sometimes as the result of the mistake of one person. I believe it should be obvious the Lord God of the Old Testament was not always the Lord God of the New Testament. Never once did our Father in heaven, while our Lord Christ Jesus walked this Earth, ask him to strike down anyone or have a disobedient village destroyed. Instead, when two of our Lord Christ Jesus' own disciples asked him if they should call upon our Father to have an evil village burned, Christ Jesus turned and sternly rebuked them. Below are the telling holy Scriptures.

Luke 9:53-55

"But the people of the village did not welcome Jesus because he was on his way to Jerusalem. When James and John saw this, they said to Jesus, 'Lord, should we call down fire from heaven to burn them up?' But Jesus turned and rebuked them'"(NLT).

I believe it is important to illustrate the mind set of James and John even at this time in their discipleship, so I would like to include another verse to show what our Lord Christ Jesus said to James and John after they asked Christ Jesus, should we call on the Lord God to send down fire from heaven to burn the village alive which had just rejected them. Here is that verse, which some manuscripts include and is included in the footnotes of my copy of the holy Scriptures.

Note: Some manuscripts add an expanded conclusion to Luke 9 verse 55 and additional sentence in Luke 9 verse 56, which reads:

"And he said, 'You don't realize what your hearts are like. For the Son of Man has not come to destroy people's lives, but to save them'"(NLT).

Is it not a bit disconcerting to know that James and John were ready and willing to have the Lord God destroy a village by burning the people alive even though there are innocent babies and children living in this village? And this, even though they are disciples of our Lord Christ Jesus.

Still, these verses show us our Father in heaven is not like the Lord God portrayed in the Old Testament where such wanton mass murder did happen. Instead, it demonstrates our Father, who speaks through our Lord Christ Jesus, will allow His children to reject Him and still not seek vengeance upon them for their refusal to listen to His Word. We have all been gifted with free will and are free to choose our own path in life without hindrance from our Father who created us.

Christ Jesus is an Instrument of Our Father in Heaven

Another important point to make is the humility displayed by our Lord Christ Jesus. Our Father in heaven used Christ Jesus to speak personally to His children and work His wonders through His Son. This also showed the humility of our Lord Christ Jesus to allow himself to be used as an instrument of our Father in heaven. I am sure it meant a great deal to our Father in heaven that Jesus the man allowed himself to be helpful in this way. There are many instances in the New Testament where Christ Jesus shows his humility, and that is how humble our Father is as well. After all, it was our Lord Christ Jesus who allowed himself to be nailed to the cross for our sins and was spat on and insulted along the way to Golgotha? And, yet, our Father who dwelt with our Lord Christ Jesus, allowed himself to be humiliated and then crucified to show His great love for all of His children all over the world. Can you not see how wonderful our Fathers love for us really is? He allowed His own children to put Him through a horribly painful and humbling ordeal in order to prove His love for them, and our Father never struck any of them down.

Another important subject which is missing from those who explore the holy Scripture and which some may continue to overlook, is our Father in heaven gifted His children with free will. Now, if we are given free will, then how can our Father become angry with us when we choose to follow a path which our Father did not choose for us to follow? Perhaps sadness yes, but not anger. Again, since our Father gave us free will then why is this not pointed out by scholars of the holy Scripture? Is it due to the fact the Old Testament portrays a very different Lord God than the one our Lord Christ Jesus taught us about? The Old Testament Lord God dominated his children and forced them to do horrible deeds in his name. Actions, that if they were carried out today by Israel or any nation on Earth would be roundly condemned and rightly so. Accusations of war crimes would quickly be brought to bear against said perpetrators.

Just one such atrocity by the God of the Old Testament is when he sent Israelites to slaughter a whole village of people. Men, women, and children, and all of their pets and animals and even put a torch to their village and fields full of grain. Would we tolerate such behavior today? No, we definitely would not. In fact, the world would be aghast by such an inhuman and evil act. The whole world would be deeply troubled should any nation try to exterminate an entire nation, village, or town anywhere in the world like that today. This shows just how far we have come spiritually from acting in such an inhuman way.

Let me give you some of the holy Scripture found in the Old Testament which demonstrate the mass killings that, allegedly, our Lord God sent the Israelites to carry out. First, we begin with this quote from the Book of Numbers.

Number 21:2-3

"Then the people of Israel made this vow to the Lord: 'If you will hand these people over to us, we will completely destroy all their towns.' The Lord heard the Israelites' request and gave them victory over the Canaanites. The Israelites completely destroyed them and their towns, and the place has been called Hormah ever since"(NLT).

Hormah means destruction. Below is another horrible act of mass murder. This one in the Book of Numbers as well.

Numbers 31:17-18

"So kill all the boys and all the women who have had intercourse with a man. Only the young girls who are virgins may live; you may keep them for yourselves"(NLT).

Another horrifying massacre by Israel was in Joshua 8: 25-26. In that massacre the Israelite army slaughtered 12,000 men, women, and children. Ai was a thriving village of mostly farmers and was happily at work the day that Israelite army came upon them. The King of Ai was told by Joshua that the land of Ai belonged to them and if he did not immediately evacuate Ai he would wipe out every man, woman, child, and infant in Ai. The King of Ai said that would be impossible and said he did not have the forces available to carry out such an order. The King pleaded with Joshua to spare the women and children, but Joshua would not concede and in the end every man, woman, child, and toddler was killed unmercifully that horrible day that Ai was forevermore wiped from the face of the Earth. Joshua held out his spear to signal to his men to keep killing the people of Ai until no one was left standing. Perhaps it did not have to happen this way if only Joshua had made sure that our Lord God really wanted Joshua to kill all the people of Ai. However, Joshua did not check back with our Lord God. Would you not want to make very sure if you were given an order like Joshua allegedly received from our Lord God, that it was a valid order by asking once or twice more to have the order verified? If you were asked by our Lord God to slaughter everyone in your neighborhood, would you do it?

Much of the Book of Joseph deals with Joshua and his men marching from one town to the next and completely wiping out all the people who live there. It is hard to believe that our Lord God would allow or sanction such a mass murder of people including many thousands of innocents.

The last massacre to mention to illustrate how cruel, barbaric, and heartless the God of the Old Testament was is found in 1st Samuel.

1st Samuel 15:3
"Now go and completely destroy the entire Amalekite nation—men, women, children, babies, cattle, sheep, goats, camels, and donkeys"(NLT).

1st Samuel 15:7-8
"Then Saul slaughtered the Amalekites from Havilah all the way to Shur, east of Egypt. He captured Agag, the Amalekite king, but completely destroyed everyone else"(NLT).

Why would anyone take part in such a cruel and evil massacre? Probably only someone who truly believed they were following the commands of the God they believed in. He may have thought, if God was willing to destroy even the innocent children and animals, what would he do to me if I disobeyed?

We should not accept the horrible behavior of the Old Testament God and should question his outrageous behavior which is inhuman at many times. To accept the belief that our Father, the creator of us all, is behind all of the horrors in the Old Testament is a mistake. The belief by many that our Lord God is responsible for all the horrors that occur on a daily basis on Earth has its roots in the Old Testament belief in an angry and vengeful God. Our Lord Christ Jesus himself has said that Satan is the ruler of this world and it takes someone even stronger to tie up a strongman like Satan and plunder his goods. This exact quote is just below.

Matthew 12:28-29

"But if I am casting out demons by the Spirit of God, then the Kingdom of God has arrived among you. For who is powerful enough to enter the house of a strong man and plunder his goods? Only someone even stronger-someone who could tie him up and then plunder his house"(NLT).

Our Lord Christ Jesus Has Arrived in Satan's House

Does this holy Scripture not imply that our Lord Christ Jesus has arrived in Satan's house and is plundering his goods? Of course, Satan's house is Earth and our Lord Christ Jesus is plundering Satan's disciples, which are his goods, and making them his own.

Still, the belief the Lord God is the ruler of this world makes it nearly impossible to question the legitimacy of the God of the Old Testament. The God of the Old Testament is a God that caused great destruction, death, and unmerciful killing of even small babies and children. This is something our Father in heaven and our Lord Christ Jesus would never think of doing. Our Father loves the little children and you had better not mess with them. Our Lord Christ Jesus shows us throughout his life that our Father is a very loving Lord God and a very humble Father and there is no "evil" in Him. Let us not forget that our Father allowed His son to be nailed to the cross and permitted all of our Fathers children living in Israel to hurl insults at him, throw stones at him, and allowed them to spit upon His Son and laugh at him and accuse him of blasphemy and throw dirt in his mouth and in his eyes, all the while our Father did not stop them from doing so. Would an arrogant Lord God stand for that kind of mistreatment of His son? No, absolutely not. Instead, he would probably destroy the whole lot of them. And our Father allowed Christ Jesus to be nailed to the cross and to suffer the way he did and be humiliated the way he was to show His love for us all. And, to ensure that anyone who accepted our Lord Christ Jesus would be able once again to return to heaven and live with our Father, our Lord Christ Jesus, The Holy Spirit and all of our friends we left behind so very long ago.

This we know as well. Our Lord Christ Jesus was a very humble man all of his 33 years on Earth. Even when he was being nailed to the cross he never spoke an ill word to anyone. Nor did he threaten to destroy his enemies by calling on our Lord God to do that very thing. And, yet, we are expected to believe the God of the Old Testament is the same Lord God we know and love in the New Testament. It does not seem possible.

Then who was this God of the Old Testament. The people of Israel it seems, were always preparing for war every Spring as if war was expected and soon they would be called to battle to destroy another village or nation living close by. This illustrates that the God they normally worshiped and feared was a vengeful, cruel, and no so loving god. Unlike the one our Lord Christ Jesus taught us. Remember what our Lord Christ Jesus said to John and Peter; "I came to save lives, not destroy them."

We Have a Free Will

Let me say this about our Lord God. He believes in freedom and will not impose His will over our own will or anyone else's. Many may find this difficult to accept since we are told often by the Churches we attend that the Lord God directs our life and whatever happens in our life is our Lord God's will. However, if the Lord God did not allow freedom of will, then we would in effect, be slaves, which again, our Father does not want for us. He wants us to be free and to be able to make decisions we believe to be in our best interest. Our Father granted us free will which makes it possible for us to freely accept our Father, or not to accept our Father. Our Father wants us to return to Him freely without duress. Only then will we really respect our Father and love Him with all of our heart, with all of our mind, and with all of our strength.

Remember the parable of the prodigal son? Did his father try to stop his son from doing what he wanted to do? No, he gave his son half his wealth and when his son had squandered his wealth and could find nothing to eat, he finally returned to his father's house and begged for forgiveness. How did his father treat him? He was as happy as a Lark upon hearing of the return of his wayward son. The father was so happy that he threw a huge feast for all of his friends and family just to welcome his son home again. He loved his wayward son that much. This is what our father will do for us once we return home to Him.

Our Father in Heaven Did Not Offer Us a False Choice

One other important matter to point out which is rarely mentioned is the principal of a false choice. A false choice would be if our Father had said we can worship Satan, or we can worship Him. That would give us only two choices, we either worship Satan or we worship our Father in heaven. However, unless we have a third choice then we are given a false choice. Either of the first two choices would force us to either be slaves of Satan or be slaves of our Lord God. However, our Lord God saw fit to give us the gift of free will when He first created us. We all have free will, therefore, since our Father gifted us with free will then we are free to choose a different path from what our Father would hope we followed and He will not hold it against us. The Constitution of the United States takes its roots from the freedom given to us by our Lord God. Christianity is based on personal freedom and choice. Our Father would not have it otherwise. Else, it would not truly be free will. Our Lord God wanted us to have free will so we could choose to worship Him freely. Our Father did not want His children to feel obligated to worship Him or demand of them to do so. Remember, our Father is a very humble Lord God as we mentioned earlier. The Lord God did not want to impose His will upon us and force us to do His will. He wanted us to freely love Him and accept His will in our lives. It was our Fathers vision from the beginning to allow us to live free and make our own choices. No matter where that might lead us. Also, without free will we would then be forced to worship Him even if we felt He did not earn our worship. For example, if we did not 'know' that Satan was the ruler of this world and Satan caused a great catastrophe and all of our family perished in said catastrophe would we still want to worship our Lord God? Perhaps not, and you would probably want to know why it was necessary they died the way they did. However, let us keep in mind that Satan is the ruler of this world and causes widespread destruction and devastation whenever he wants, it is not our Father who is responsible for the death and destruction we see every day in our world.

Punishment Does Not Come Before Judgment

Our Lord Christ Jesus emphasized that we should always put others before ourselves and be willing to give the shirt off our backs if someone should ask us for it. This is not the kind of Lord God we find in the Book of Revelation. Instead, we find a very vengeful and wrathful god who is willing to destroy the whole Earth to exact his vengeance upon the entire human race. Including the birds of the air, the fish and mammals on land, sea, and in the oceans, and the animals, birds, and insects living on the ground or in the air. Also, is not this punishment being exacted before judgement day? Yes, it is and that should also tell us this is something a 'just' Lord God would not do. Punishment does not come before Judgement. Also, it must be said our Father loves us more than we could possibly love one another. In fact, if our Father had his druthers He would not allow a single one of His children to perish. This is difficult for us to believe, after all, we have learned since we were youngsters in Sunday School and up to the present time that the Lord God is a vengeful and angry Lord God. And, we also discover our Lord God is rather fickle as well. However, our Lord Christ Jesus came to Earth to reveal to us our true Father in heaven and he did so throughout his 33 years of life on Earth. Our Lord Christ Jesus was a sweet, kind, friendly, caring, sympathetic, tender, and merciful person just as is our Father in heaven. This is what we should remember as we read the Book of Revelation and discover in Revelation the return of the god of the Old Testament. Anyway, that is all I have to say at this point concerning our true Lord God.

CHAPTER 1

The Vision

John starts out in the Book of Revelation by writing that our Lord God gave our Lord Christ Jesus a vision who then passed this vision on to an angel who then presented the vision to John. It is hard to imagine how a vision can be passed from one person to another. For most of us all we can do is recall the vision the best our memory will allow and then convey what we have seen to the best of our ability with words only. However, for Christ Jesus and the angel, they will be able to remember exactly what the vision looked like and even convey it to John exactly as the angel had first seen it. However, John was not able to remember exactly what the angel had shown him since his brain was made of flesh and not as receptive as the mind of an angel or the mind of our Lord Christ Jesus which is spirit. Inevitably, John made some mistakes in translation and was influenced by the mind of a fallen archangel by the name of Satan. Other apostles were also influenced by Satan and made errors in the holy Scripture they wrote down as well.

Fortunately for the other apostles, they were able to compare what they remember of our Lord Christ Jesus' teachings and were then able to cross check each other's writing and make corrections in the holy Scripture they authored. Still, errors in the text they wrote still occurred and we can still recognize them to this day.

Here is a case in point. Paul wrote the following in 1st Timothy 2:14-15.

1st Timothy 2:14-15

"And it was not Adam who was deceived by Satan. The woman was deceived, and sin was the result. But women will be saved through childbearing, assuming they continue to live in faith, love, holiness, and modesty"(NLT).

Clearly, this is not true. Our Lord Christ Jesus made it very clear that 'everyone' who believed in him would have everlasting life. Paul, on the contrary asserts that women would be saved by "...childbearing, assuming they continue to live in faith, love, holiness, and modesty."

The holy Scripture in 1st Timothy 2:14-15 is an example of Satan at work in distorting the truth concerning the salvation of women. Paul was raised all his life as a Pharisee and he was never able to fully separate himself from it. What Paul wrote in 1st Timothy is what the Jews believed concerning women. Not what Christians of the time knew concerning the salvation of women. Women were not well respected in the Jewish faith. Men were exalted above women and often the Jewish women were treated as second class people. And, as you can see from the holy Scripture just quoted, men felt that women were to blame for what transpired in the Garden of Eden and put the blame on women for the life they were then living. This is also why Jewish men were in charge and women were under the control of their husband. This is also written of in the holy Scripture in Genesis. Here is that verse.

Genesis 3:16

"And you will desire to control your husband, but he will rule over you"(NLT).

This same belief was later passed on to the Christian faith. Does a loving Father curse His own children? This is what the god of Genesis did. I do not believe a loving Lord God would ever curse any of His children if He loves them as much as our Lord Christ Jesus tells us He does. Christ Jesus displayed our Fathers love in his own life. Over, and over again, by healing his children of their afflictions and raising them from the dead, and sacrificing himself on the cross. This to make sure his children would one day return to their Father in heaven if they would only believe in him.

Returning to John's recollection of the vision given to him by our Fathers angel. The very first contact the angel of our Lord God made with John was on the Lord's Day while John was on the Island of Patmos. John was exiled to the Island of Patmos for preaching the Word of our Lord God and for his testimony of our Lord Christ Jesus. John described the circumstances of his first contact with the angel sent by our Lord Christ Jesus with these words.

Revelation 1:10

"It was the Lord's Day, and I was worshiping in the spirit. Suddenly, I heard behind me a loud voice like a trumpet blast"(NLT).

This must have startled John terrible to suddenly hear a voice with the volume of a trumpet blast while he was worshiping in peaceful solemnity.

Revelation 1:11
"It said, 'Write in a book everything you see, and send it to the seven churches in the cities of Ephesus, Smyrna, Pergamum, Thyatira, Sardis, Philadelphia, and Laodicea'"(NLT).

When John turned to see who was speaking to him he did not behold an angel of our Lord God, instead it was a vision of seven gold lampstands with someone like the Son of Man standing in the middle of the lampstands. John then went on to describe further what he was seeing.

Revelation 1:13-16
"And standing in the middle of the lampstands was someone like the Son of Man. He was wearing a long robe with a gold sash across his chest. His head and his hair were white like wool, as white as snow. And his eyes were like flames of fire. His feet were like polished bronze refined in a furnace, and his voice thundered like mighty ocean waves. He held seven stars in his right hand, and a sharp two-edged sword came from his mouth. And his face was like the sun in all its brilliance"(NLT).

In the footnotes of my holy Scriptures, the New Living Translation it reads: Revelation 1:13, Or *like a son of man.* Parentheses theirs not mine.

John does not say what color of robe the Son of Man was wearing, which is a bit curious. It should have been a brilliant white robe as a symbol of the Son of Man's purity of heart and purpose. John also described the Son of Man as having a thunderous voice, yet John did not say what the Son of Man said to him. Also, notice that John says it was "someone like the Son of Man." John did not say it 'was' the Son of Man who John clearly knew. And, the text just above read: *'like a son of man.'*

Revelation Revealed: A Modern Interpretation

Throughout the Book of Revelation, the use of symbolism conveys much of what is not written and, therefore, makes it difficult to understand and interpret. Symbolism is something most of us in the Western world have trouble with since our written language rarely uses symbology. Our society does use symbols like emoji's and signs that warn us with symbols, such as the symbol for a radiation hazard or high voltage hazard. We know immediately from the design of the symbol used they mean danger. Other places where symbolism is used are Stop signs, Caution signs, and Road Hazard signs, which we have all learned to understand with merely a glance. Just those few words make us take notice and understand almost immediately there is an intersection immediately ahead and we should begin to slow down in order to make the stop. I instinctively look in my rearview mirror to make sure anyone behind me is slowing down as well. So, with just the appearance of the symbol we have learned to picture in our mind the sequence of steps we should take to avoid the upcoming hazard.

However, symbology was very common in centuries past and it helped to convey meaning to people who did not share a common language. Symbolism actually came before written language. In the Book of Revelation, we will find complex symbology and even numerology which some regard as an Occult science. Still, it is hard to overlook the numerals we will see. It will become obvious as we progress though Revelation that numbers do have meaning and we will explore just what they mean for good or for bad. Unfortunately, we do not have the equivalence of a Rosetta Stone to help us interpret the meaning of the symbology we will come across in the pages ahead, or even the meaning of some numbers that are used in this text.

CHAPTER 2

The Book of Revelation Begins

In chapter 2, the first Church mentioned in the book of Revelation is Ephesus, then Smyrna, Pergamum, and Thyatira. Pergamum was considered the capital of Satan's power in Asia Minor by our Lord Christ Jesus.

To the Church in Ephesus

The Church in Ephesus is threatened with the removal of our Lord God's protection. This would not be a good thing. However, there was one thing they had going for them and that was they did not love the Nicolaitans, which our Lord Christ Jesus praised them for.

To the Church in Smyrna

To the Church in Smyrna our Lord Christ Jesus said this.

Revelation 2:9-11

"I know about your suffering and your poverty--but you are rich! I know the blasphemy of those opposing you. They say they are Jews, but they are not, because their synagogue belongs to Satan. Don't be afraid of what you are about to suffer. The devil will throw some of you into prison to test you. You will suffer for ten days. But if you remain faithful even when facing death, I will give you the crown of life.

"Anyone with ears to hear must listen to the Spirit and understand what he is saying to the Churches. Whoever is victorious will not be harmed by the second death"(NLT).

The second death is burning in hell.

To the Church in Pergamum

Apostle John wrote a letter on behalf of our Lord Christ Jesus to the Church at Pergamum which mentions a white stone. Some scholars have speculated the stone might instead be a white pearl. Which would you rather have, a white stone or a white pearl?

Our Lord Christ Jesus said this to the Church in Pergamum.

Revelation 2:13-16

"I know that you live in the city where Satan has his throne, yet you have remained loyal to me. You refused to deny me even when Antipas, my faithful witness, was martyred among you there in Satan's city.

"But I have a few complaints against you. You tolerate some among you whose teaching is like that of Balaam, who showed Balak how to trip up the people of Israel. He taught them to sin by eating food offered to idols and by committing sexual

sin. In a similar way, you have some Nicolaitans among you who follow the same teaching. Repent of your sin, or I will come to you suddenly and fight against them with the sword of my mouth"(NLT).

In the above paragraphs our Lord Christ Jesus said Pergamum had Satan's throne there and was considered Satan's city. How would you feel if our Lord Christ Jesus said this about your city? What a difficult challenge it must have been for the first Christians in Pergamum.

What if you were in Pergamum at the time John brought this letter to your Church to read and you heard Christ Jesus himself might show up to fight Nicolaitans in person? You would probably want to see our Lord Christ Jesus showing up just so you could see him in person. And, to hear him personally chastise the Nicolaitans among them. I believe I probably would like to have seen Christ Jesus show up to chastise the Nicolaitans myself. So, is this a real threat or not?

Revelation 2:17

"Anyone with ears to hear musts listen to the Spirit and understand what he is saying to the churches. To everyone who is victorious I will give some of the manna that has been hidden away in heaven. And I will give to each one a white stone, and on the stone will be engraved a new name that no one understands except the one who receives it"(NLT).

What might this white stone represent if only the one who receives it can read the name on it? Does it mean even our Lord Christ Jesus cannot read the name inscribed on it? It does say, "...on the stone will be engraved a new name that no one understands except the one who receives it." What does this phrase mean? Once again, we are confronted with something that escapes interpretation. Should we take this phrase seriously. Or, is this phrase only meant to confound and confuse us? Perhaps it is a beautiful and a very special gift for those who remain faithful. What might a beautiful white stone look like in heaven? Perhaps more dazzlingly beautiful than we can imagine. And, the name on the stone will be known only by the one receiving it. This would make it a very personal gift and an intimate gift as well?

To the Church in Thyatira

Our Lord Christ Jesus said the following.

Revelation 2:18
"Write this letter to the angel of the church in Thyatira. This is the message from the Son of God, whose eyes are like flames of fire, whose feet are like polished bronze..."(NLT).

Does the above verse sound like something Christ Jesus might look like? Why would he appear with flames of fire emanating from his eyes? Or, having feet like polished bronze? This description does not remind us of our Lord Christ Jesus at all, from what we have read of him in the New Testament. Here, he is being presented as some frightening being instead of a very approachable person with a very peaceful disposition. Why would he not simply appear as in the New Testament wearing a robe, belt, and sandals. Christ Jesus was always a humble person and now in the Book of Revelation he is made to seem foreboding and frightening. We should probably doubt this description of our Lord Christ Jesus as factual.

Revelation 2:19
"I know all the things you do. I have seen your love, your faith, your service, and your patient endurance. And I can see your constant improvement in all these things"(NLT).

Revelation 2:20-21

"But I have this complaint against you. You are permitting that woman-that Jezebel who calls herself a prophet-to lead my servants astray. She teaches them to commit sexual sin and to eat food offered to idols. I gave her time to repent, but she does not want to turn away from her immorality"(NLT).

Revelation 2:22-23

"Therefore, I will throw her on a bed of suffering, and those who commit adultery with her will suffer greatly unless they repent and turn away from her evil deeds. I will strike her children dead. Then all the churches will know that I am the one who searches out the thoughts and intentions of every person. And I will give to each of you whatever you deserve"(NLT).

The holy Scripture just above from Christ Jesus is not what me might expect from him. For one thing, our Lord Christ Jesus would not call a woman a Jezebel which is a derogatory term. Certainly, Christ Jesus would not refer to anyone in a derogatory way. Which is calling someone a dirty name. Also, the idea that our Lord God or our Lord Christ Jesus would kill innocent children in order to punish their parents flies in the face of our Fathers especial love for children. Christ Jesus has a special place in his heart for children as well. Also, we must consider this a threat since our Lord Christ Jesus allegedly said that "And I will give to each of you whatever you deserve." Does that not sound like a threat? Again, this is something which our Lord Christ Jesus would not do and never did in the New Testament.

Further down in the above quoted Scripture we read that, supposedly, Christ Jesus searches the thoughts and intentions of every person. Again, this is something our Lord Christ Jesus would not do since it would be a violation of said persons privacy. One thing I have learned since my own encounter with Satan and his demons is our

Lord Christ Jesus and The Holy Spirit are the most polite, respectful, caring, and well-mannered people you will ever meet. They do not address anyone with a derogatory name or threaten me or anyone else. Satan, on the other hand was always accusing our Lord God's angels for doing one thing or another.

Our Father in Heaven, Our Lord Christ Jesus, and The Holy Spirit Are the Politest People You Will Ever Meet

I know it is hard to believe, but whenever I spoke with either Christ Jesus or The Holy Spirit they never were impolite to me or to anyone we may have spoken about whether that person was a bad person from my perspective or a good person from my perspective. And, they were never upset with me no matter what I might think or say. It was like a very wise person speaking to a very young child and not wanting to hurt the child's feelings. They would very lovingly tell me what I just said was not a very nice thing to say. I love that person very much. You should be more respectful of others and try to understand who they are. Also, they always spoke respectfully of everyone because they love everyone so very much. Our Lord Christ Jesus and The Holy Spirit would correct me if I did speak ill of someone, but in a polite way. Imagine if someone spoke ill of your child. Would you not be a little upset about it, especially when they spoke ill of your children in your presence? This is why the Lord Christ Jesus, The Holy Spirit, and even our Lord God expects us to respect and love each and every one we come in contact with.

One very important reason we should respect and treat everyone politely is that each of us have lived many lives and have done horrible things in the many lives we have lived on Earth. So, even though we may be a reasonably good person in our eyes and perhaps in our neighbors' eyes we have done horrible things in our past lives. We have all done wrong in the past and so we should not be so quick to judge others who we feel are doing wrong today. We have all accumulated so many sins in our many lifetimes on Earth that we could never possibly make up for them no matter how good we might be. The worst of us today will one day grow spiritually and be a much better person in some future lifetime. However, this does not mean they will not possibly end up in hell. Satan is the one who casts people into hell and he is pretty much free to do so to anyone he chooses except those who are very strong disciples of our Lord Christ Jesus. This is what we should keep in mind before condemning someone too harshly. Naturally, we should not allow them to continue to harm others since that would be disrespectful to others who may suffer due to their selfish acts or lustful desires. We should not allow this bad person to continue to do harm to others since we would then be ignoring our Lord Christ Jesus command to love one another and protect one another.

Christ Jesus accepts us as his disciple even though we may stray from his teachings. If we should ever stray from his teachings, then our Lord Christ Jesus will do all he can to bring us back into his fold. Did Christ Jesus not say in effect he will leave the ninety-nine sheep and go after the one which has strayed and when he finds it he will rejoice and celebrate his new-found stray sheep? This is why we should not believe what we have just read concerning the Church in Thyatira.

Keep in mind that Satan will even condemn himself if necessary to cause us to stray and this is what he is doing with this quote, *"(deeper truths, as they call them-depths of Satan actually.)"* Please read the paragraph below carefully.

Revelation 2:24-28

"But I also have a message for the rest of you in Thyatira who have not followed this false teaching (deeper truths, as they call them-depths of Satan actually). I will ask nothing more of you except that you hold tightly to what you have until I come. To all who are victorious, who obey me to the very end. To them I will give authority over all the nations. They will rule the nations with an iron rod and smash them like clay pots. They will have the same authority I received from my Father, and I will also give them the morning star"!(NLT).

In the above verse Satan is condemning himself just to lead us astray. And then Satan goes on to quote from the Old Testament. The quote above is partially taken from the below quote from Psalms. Compare the two and see what you believe.

Psalms 2:7-9

"The king proclaims the Lord's decree: 'The Lord said to me, You are my son. Today I have become your father. Only ask, and I will give you the nations as your inheritance, the whole earth as your possession. You will break them with an iron rod and smash them like clay pots.'"

Does this sound like our Father in heaven or Satan? Why would our Lord God give Christ Jesus the authority to "...break them with an iron rod and smash them like clay pots?" Here, the supposed Lord God we all know and love is giving our Lord Christ Jesus the authority to destroy completely any nation on Earth that he wishes to. This is a very violent thing, to destroy a nation, and not something our Lord God would ever do since He loves all of His children on Earth. Christ Jesus once told James and John that he came to Earth to save lives, not to destroy them. Therefore, it must be Satan who inserted this bit of

Scripture into the holy Scripture to distort the truth of our Lord Christ Jesus and our Lord God as well. Does this not sound similar to what the God of the Old Testament said to the twelve tribes of Israel? The Israelites will be given dominion of all the people of the Promised Land and they are commanded to march through the heathen villages and slaughter everyone because they were such evil people. And, this was commanded by the God they believed in. However, was it our Lord God?

CHAPTER 3

To the Churches in Sardis, Philadelphia, and Laodicea

I n this chapter three, we are again confronted with the number 7. For instance, Revelation 3:1 states the following.

Revelation 3:1
"Write this letter to the angel of the church in Sardis. This is the message from the one who has the sevenfold Spirit of God and the seven stars..."(NLT).

There is no further mention of 7 after this beginning verse. However, it has been determined that our Lord God has 9 aspects and not 7 which was addressed in the Introduction to this book. Let me mention once again that the Holy Trinity is represented by the number 3 and the multiples of 3 which are 6, 9, and 12. I refer to them as the holy numbers. The 9 aspects of our Lord God are these;

15

love, mercy, grace, forgiveness, wisdom, patience, kindness, compassion, and justice. This shows our Lord God has 9 aspects and not 7 as is written in the first verse of chapter 3. And, what are those 7 aspects which are mentioned but not given? They are pride, envy, avarice, anger, luxury, intemperance, and sloth. These are all aspects of Satan. This being said, should we accept what will follow after "the sevenfold Spirit of God and the seven stars...?" Perhaps not.

The letter to the Church in Philadelphia starts with Revelation 3:7, which reads as follows.

Revelation 3:7

"Write this letter to the angel of the church in Philadelphia. This is the message from the one who is holy and true, the one who has the key of David. What he opens, no one can close; and what he closes, no one can open..."(NLT).

Then there is the letter to the Church in Laodicea which begins in this way.

Revelation 3:14

"Write this letter to the angel of the church in Laodicea. This is the message from the one who is the Amen-the faithful and true witness, the beginning of God's new creation..."(NLT).

Both of these remaining two letters can be read and seen to contain no 7s so they are most likely true. All we seem to have here is letters to each Church praising and chastising them for the good they have done and the not so good things. Our Lord Christ Jesus is trying to guide them in the right direction and telling his Church what their reward will be if they do not stray from his teachings. Let us pause a minute and try to imagine what it must have been like for the seven Churches in Asia Minor which received a letter from our Lord Christ Jesus.

Let us imagine John the Apostle walking into each of the seven Churches and presenting them with a letter from our Lord Christ Jesus. What a surprise it must have been, for John to tell each congregation an angel of the Lord God asked him to write this Church a letter sent from our Lord Christ Jesus. What would we do today if someone with the authority of John were to walk into our holy Church and present the pastor, minister, or priest a letter addressed to them by our Lord Christ Jesus? Might we suddenly feel a lump in our throats knowing the letter may contain some criticism of the way our Church is being managed? This would be a very serious matter and we would want to correct our mistakes right away. It would actually be a Blessing if every Church of our Lord Christ Jesus were to receive such a letter, since then each Church of our Lord God would be able to know exactly where they are failing and where they are doing good. It would help the Churches know if they are going in the right direction. Also, from the letter, they would know how to correct their path so they could be sure they were going in the right direction. Now, suppose you were a member of some Church and the pastor, minister, or priest got up and stood before the congregation on Sunday morning and read aloud the letter they recently received from our Lord Christ Jesus. Would we not be very attentive to what was read, much as the seven Churches in Asia Minor must have been. I am sure that would be the situation. And, we might find we must make some corrections in our own lives which may or may not be so easy to make. On the other hand, to receive a letter from our Lord Christ Jesus praising us for our good works would be very exciting and joyous. We might leave our Church feeling much better than we have felt in a long time and our faith would be strengthened as well.

What Does Seven Mean?

In this chapter 4, we see several times that the number 7 is used once again. Therefore, we should not take seriously anything written in these pages found in chapter four. For example, in verse 5 it reads as follows.

Revelation 4:5
"From the throne came flashes of lightning and the rumble of thunder. And in front of the throne were seven torches with burning flames. This is the sevenfold Spirit of God"(NLT).

And it continues with,

Revelation 4:6
"In front of the throne was a shiny sea of glass, sparkling like crystal"(NLT).

Does the description of the sea of glass not make you cringe a bit? It does me since I would never want to go swimming in a sea of glass. The image of a sea of glass does not sound beautiful at all, only dangerous with waves of sharp glass pounding the beach. Especially, when you consider this scene is supposed to be of heaven. How beautiful can you make a sea of glass? I doubt there is a single shard of glass in heaven. Does this image of a sea of glass inspire you with beauty? So, you see, this is just another odd image we are expected to accept as a possible view our Lord God would have in front of his throne in heaven. Can you think of a more beautiful scene? I believe I could.

We have already discussed that our Lord God does not have 7 aspects; however, Satan does so we must be cautious what we read with 7 in the holy Scripture.

The Printing Press Was Invented Some 800 Years After the Passing of Apostle John

Then, as John continued putting down everything he saw and heard on parchment paper, the Book of Revelation slowly took form. After making a complete copy of what he had heard and saw in his vision, John made 7 additional copies, one for each of the 7 Churches in Asia Minor. It was a long time before John was ready to deliver the manuscripts relating the Book of Revelation. All of the Churches in Asia Minor were very pleased to read the holy Scripture provided by John. Each of the 7 Churches our Lord Christ Jesus asked John to deliver a copy of the Book of Revelation to, which included an accompanying letter, received their copy in person by John the Apostle. Each Church was then able to teach the holy Scripture of the Book of Revelation. In fact, many neighboring Churches sent representatives to any of the 7 Churches in Asia Minor and made their own copies of the Book of Revelation by sitting down and hand copying it letter by letter and number by number. However, there were some minor variations brought about by hand writing each copy; however, it was the only way it could be done during that period of time. Things would begin to change in the task of copying in due time; but, it would be long after John finished writing the Book of Revelation. The printing press would be designed and invented in China approximately 800 years after John's demise on Earth. Up until that time the only option was to hand copy text and repeat the process over and over so that others could also read and learn of new things. This made books available mostly to the very rich, and only close friends were allowed to borrow the books. They would then go and tell others about what they had read. Only very good story tellers were allowed to read the books owned by the very rich in order to convey the most accurate account of the story or information they just completed reading. In this way, the people would get a better idea what was really written in the pages of said book.

The Scroll with Seven Seals

In this chapter 5 of the Book of Revelation we see again the liberal use of the number 7. It is used in the very first verse of chapter 5 and it reads as follows.

Revelation 5:1

"Then I saw a scroll in the right hand of the one who was sitting on the throne. There was writing on the inside and the outside of the scroll, and it was sealed with seven seals"(NLT).

Then in the next paragraph we find 7 once again.

Revelation 5:5

"But one of the twenty-four elders said to me. 'Stop weeping! Look, the Lion of the tribe of Judah, the heir to David's throne, has won the victory. He is worthy to open the scroll and its seven seals'"(NLT).

Christ Jesus Heir to David's Throne

Can you imagine how our Lord Christ Jesus would be heir to David's throne? This would make King David appear to be greater than our Lord Christ Jesus, which is definitely not the case. Why would our Lord Christ Jesus be heir to an earthly throne? Christ Jesus is the head of our Lord God's Church on Earth, our Lord God's earthly Kingdom; but, this is not the same as sitting on David's throne. Our Father's Kingdom is a spiritual kingdom. Also, remember, our Lord Christ Jesus was not fathered by King David's linage. Christ Jesus was born by immaculate conception and not fathered by earthly man. Lastly, in verse 6 we have this strange description of Christ Jesus.

Revelation 5:6-7

"Then I saw a Lamb that looked as if it had been slaughtered, but it was now standing between the throne and the four living beings, and among the twenty-four elders. He had seven horns and seven eyes, which represents the sevenfold Spirit of God that is sent out into every part of the earth. He stepped forward and took the scroll from the right hand of the one sitting on the throne"(NLT).

Does it not seem odd that our Lord Christ Jesus would first start out as a Lamb that looked as if it had been slaughtered, with seven horns and seven eyes and then be handed a scroll to read. It also states the 7 horns and 7 eyes represent the sevenfold Spirit of our Lord God once again. It has already been established that our Lord God has 9 spirits, not 7. Therefore, the remainder of this chapter should be set aside. Let us now move on to chapter 6.

The First Six Seals Are Opened

In this chapter 6, John tells us of the beginnings of the trials and tribulations which will befall those living on Earth. John begins by saying this was all given to him in a vision. Can you imagine what a vision must look like that actually gives us so many details concerning what is taking place? It must be a very spectacular vision with all the different scenes and hearing all the instructions given to the angelic angels to do this and then that and so forth. For example, do you remember the time when John described how Satan went after mother Mary and her baby Jesus? Satan tried to devour baby Jesus even before he was born. This will be described in more detail later in chapter 12. How did Satan know that baby Jesus had been born on Earth? I think it had to do with the fact that Satan can read the stars which contain some of the history of Earth from the beginning of time. This as well will be covered in chapter 12. Let us begin with the first paragraph in this chapter and analyze each paragraph.

Revelation 6:1-2

"As I watched, the Lamb broke the first of the seven seals on the scroll. Then I heard one of the four living beings say with a voice like thunder, 'Come!' I looked up and saw a white horse standing there. Its rider carried a bow, and a crown was placed on his head. He rode out to win many battles and gain the victory."

Now, does this verse tell us much? It seems to infer the rider on the white horse may represent our Lord Christ Jesus with the sentence, "He rode out to win many battles and gain the victory." However, is the victory already not his when he was sacrificed on the cross at Golgotha? This is what we have been told and I am sure it is the truth. Now read paragraph two of chapter 6.

Revelation 6:3-4

"When the Lamb broke the second seal, I heard the second living being say, 'Come!' Then another horse appeared, a red one. Its rider was given a mighty sword and the authority to take peace from the earth. And there was war and slaughter everywhere."

Here is where the horrors begin. There is war and slaughter everywhere. Imagine our Lord God giving one of his innocent angels the authority to slaughter people everywhere on Earth. Would our Father do such a thing? I doubt it very much. Satan would, however.

Revelation 6:5-6

"When the Lamb broke the third seal, I heard the third living being say, 'Come!' I looked up and saw a black horse, and its rider was holding a pair of scales in his hand. And I heard a voice from among the four living beings say, 'A loaf of wheat bread or three loaves of barley will cost a day's pay. And don't waste the olive oil and wine.'"

What are we to make of this paragraph? Again, supposedly Christ Jesus breaks the third seal to bring on more disaster upon the people of Earth. Perhaps this time famine. However, it is so difficult to imagine the kind, generous, loving, compassionate, merciful, just, gracious, forgiving, wise and patient Christ Jesus taking part in such a chamber of horrors. Worse than anything we can possibly imagine.

Revelation 6:7-8

"When the Lamb broke the fourth seal, I heard the fourth living being say, 'Come!' I looked up and saw a horse whose color was pale green. Its rider was named Death, and his companion was the Grave. These two were given authority over one-fourth of the earth, to kill with the sword and famine and disease and wild animals"(NLT).

There is little to say of the above paragraph except for one thing. The footnotes in my copy of the holy Scriptures has an asterisk beside the word grave. This footnote shows in Greek the original meaning 'was Hades' and not grave as they have in the above verse. This is one of several places in the holy Scripture that mentions the existence of hades. So, what is hades? Sometimes it is defined as the underworld or a cavern where lost Souls go to live until the return of our Lord Christ Jesus. Christ Jesus said to me that hades was a place where Souls who do not go to hell or to heaven go to rest from their last lifetime on Earth since everyone's life is always traumatic in some way and is usually very difficult. Also, after a thousand years in hell a person can then leave hell and be taken to hades to recuperate from the torment they endured before being reborn on Earth. The definition of eternity is actually a thousand-year period of time and not for all time. And, it is not our Father in heaven who sends us to hell, but Satan himself. More on this later.

Revelation 6:9-11

"When the Lamb broke the fifth seal, I saw under the altar the souls of all who had been martyred for the word of God and for being faithful in their testimony. They shouted to the Lord and said, 'O Sovereign Lord, holy and true, how long before you judge the people who belong to this world and avenge our blood for what they have done to us?' Then a white robe was given to each of them. And they were told to rest a little longer until the full number of their brothers and sisters-their fellow servants of Jesus who were to be martyred-had joined them"(NLT).

Here we have a situation where those who are dead are asking our Lord Christ Jesus to avenge their blood for what was done to them. This is not what Christ Jesus would do since he loves everyone. Even those who commit very bad acts. Also, the people under the Alter are all going to heaven due to the fact they were all martyred for our Lord Christ Jesus, so why would revenge be on their minds now? It is not in our Lord Christ Jesus' character to seek revenge, but instead to forgive and move on. So, here is another instance in the Book of Revelation we are reminded of the ways of the God in the Old Testament who is betrayed as being vengeful, angry, and cruel. Now, on to the sixth seal.

This was the worst day the Earth has ever seen. It was a day of great fear and trepidation. Most of the people of Earth did not understand what was happening to them. All of a sudden, terrible events were happening that were killing thousands of people. All of the available resources to care for the homeless and injured had been exhausted weeks ago, yet, almost every day brought another horrible disaster. Those who were still alive and uninjured struggled to care for all of those who had no home, no food, and hardly any clothes. The children were everyone's first priority and keeping them alive and sheltered was their main concern. What else could possibly happen they asked themselves each time another catastrophe occurred. What was our Lord God in heaven doing to help us, they continued to ask themselves? It was as though their Lord God had completely abandoned them and was now punishing them for who knows what. Their fear was so great they actually called on the mountains and rocks to cover them up from the next catastrophe which seemed inevitable. Even the kings of the Earth, the rulers and generals, the wealthy and the powerful, slaves and free people, all cried to the rocks of the mountains to cover them up and protect them from the wrath of our Lord Christ Jesus which had finally arrived. Who could escape his wrath?

The paragraph above shows that whoever wrote this part of the Book of Revelation intended to accuse our Father in heaven and our Lord Christ Jesus as being angry and full of wrath when they are both completely the opposite. Here we have the Lamb, our Lord Christ Jesus, accused of being about to display his wrath and everyone is so frightened they call on the mountains and the rocks to fall on them to hide them from the great wrath which is about to unfold. However, why would they be so frightened of our Lord Christ Jesus? He is the sweetest, the kindest, and the most caring person you would ever want to meet, and as gentle as a Lamb, and yet they are terrified of his alleged wrath. Another symbol of our Lord Christ Jesus is the Lamb. Can you imagine an angry little lamb? Can you imagine the kind of wrath that a lamb could bring forth? It makes me smile to imagine a little lamb in a wrathful state of mind. They love to kick their little heals in the air and pretend to be so big and dangerous, yet they are about as cuddly and cute at they get. This is why we should not take the above holy Scripture seriously. I try to imagine our loving and kind and graceful Lord Jesus angry enough to frighten people so badly they would ask for the rocks and mountains to fall on them to protect them from our Lord Christ Jesus' wrath, and I cannot image it.

CHAPTER 7

The Twelve Tribes
of Israel

In this chapter 7, we read of 144,000 Israelites from the twelve tribes of Israel who received the seal of God on their foreheads.

Revelation 7:3-4

"Wait! Don't harm the land or the sea or the trees until we have placed the seal of God on the foreheads of his servants.

"And I heard how many were marked with the seal of God-144,000 were sealed from all the tribes of Israel..."(NLT).

Now, what is missing from this description of who is marked with the seal of our Lord God? There are no Christians mentioned, although, some, if not most of those mentioned coming from all the tribes of Israel might be Christians. However, we cannot be sure and it does not mention anyone being marked with the seal of our Lord God outside of the tribes of Israel who may be Christian.

Only those within the tribes of Israel. Why would the angels sent by our Lord God not also place the seal of our Father on all the Christians as well? In fact, throughout the Book of Revelation, there is hardly any mention of Christians. This is a bit curious. There are far more Christians outside of Israel than inside of Israel. So, why are Christians not being given the seal of our Lord God on their foreheads? Perhaps the Book of Revelation was written more for Jews people than for Christians.

In chapter 21 we will find that the new Jerusalem will be on the new Earth. It will be there since it is known as the holy City of God. In fact, all three major religions consider Jerusalem a holy City. Still, as we will continue to find, there is very little mention of Christians in the Book of Revelation.

Revelation 7:9
"After this I saw a vast crowd, too great to count, from every nation and tribe and people and language, standing in front of the throne and before the Lamb. They were clothed in white robes and held palm branches in their hands"(NLT).

Then John speaks of a vast crowd of people too great to count. They were standing in front of the thrown before our Lord Christ Jesus. They were all clothed in white robes and held palm branches in their hands. And, they were shouting with a great roar.

Revelation 7:10
"Salvation comes from our God who sits on the throne and from the Lamb!"(NLT).
Revelation 7:13-17
"Then one of the twenty-four elders asked me. 'Who are these who are clothed in white? Where did they come from?'

"And I said to him, 'Sir you are the one who knows.'

"Then he said to me, 'These are the ones who died in the great tribulation. They have washed their robes in the blood of the Lamb and made them white. That is why they stand in front of God's throne and serve him day and night in his Temple. And he who sits on the throne will give them shelter. They will never again be hungry or thirsty; they will never be scorched by the heat of the sun. For the Lamb on the throne will be their Shepherd. He will lead them to springs of life-giving water. And God will wipe every tear from their eyes'"(NLT).

More Concerning the Seven Seals

In this chapter 8 there are several uses of the number 7 and throughout this chapter we are given descriptions of catastrophes let loose upon the people of Earth where 7 is seen in the Book of Revelation. It is a horrible time of death, destruction, and great anguish throughout the world. And, I am sure, not the doing of our Lord God in heaven who loves us dearly. Satan is the one who relishes in death, destruction, and great anguish. For example, in the very first verse we have 7 used three times. Here is the first verse.

Revelation 8:1-2

"When the Lamb broke the seventh seal on the scroll, there was silence throughout heaven for about half an hour. I saw the seven angels who stand before God, and they were given seven trumpets"(NLT).

Here we see that it is supposedly our Lord Christ Jesus who breaks the 7th seal and begins another catastrophic event upon the people of Earth.

Revelation 8:6-7
"Then the seven angels with the seven trumpets prepared to blow their mighty blasts.

"The first angel blew his trumpet, and hail mixed with blood were thrown down on the earth. One third of the earth was set on fire, one-third of the trees were burned, and all the green grass burned"(NLT).

Revelation 8:8-9
"Then the second angel blew his trumpet, and a great mountain of fire was thrown into the sea. One-third of the water is the sea became blood, one-third of all things living in the sea died, and one-third of all the ships on the sea were destroyed"(NLT).

Revelation 8:10-11
"Then the third angel blew his trumpet, and a great star fell from the sky, burning like a torch. It fell on one-third of the rivers and on the springs of water. The name of the star was Bitterness. It made one-third of the water bitter, and many people died from drinking the bitter water"(NLT).

Revelation 8:12
"Then the fourth angel blew his trumpet, and one-third of the sun was struck, and one-third of the moon, and one-third of the stars, and they became dark. And one-third of the day was dark, and also one-third of the night"(NLT).

Revelation 8:13

"Then I looked, and I heard a single eagle crying loudly as it flew through the air, 'Terror, terror, terror to all who belong to this world because of what will happen when the last three angels blow their trumpets"(NLT).

What we have just read demonstrates terrible events happening on earth, supposedly, at the behest of our Lord Christ Jesus who has opened the scroll and read it aloud and then each of four angels blow their trumpets, supposedly handed to them by our Lord God, and each time a trumpet sounds more disasters appear on earth and in the heavens. Does this sound to you like the acts of a loving Lord God, or more like the acts of Satan, who we know hates humankind and would like to see all Christians wiped from the face of the Earth? This reiterates why I believe that 7 is an evil number in the context of the Book of Revelation, and is the number of Satan's worst evil traits. Why would those living in heaven act in such a horrifying way towards the people of Earth? After all, our Lord God gave us free will and should not persecute us for choosing a different path to follow. These actions we have just read from Revelation are also punishing Christians and it is written in the holy Scripture that if these days are not cut short, all of our Lord God's children will also die.

The Remaining Three Seals

I n this chapter 9, we see a continuation of the three remaining angels blowing their trumpets and catastrophe soon follows. Let us continue with the first angel blowing their trumpet and what follows.

Revelation 9:1-2

"The fifth angel blew his trumpet, and I saw a star that had fallen to earth from the sky, and he was given the key to the shaft of the bottomless pit. When he opened it, smoke poured out as though from a huge furnace, and the sunlight and air turned dark from the smoke"(NLT).

Revelation 9:3-6

"Then locusts came from the smoke and descended on the earth, and they were given power to sting like scorpions. They were told not to harm the grass or plants or trees, but only the people who did not have the seal of God on their foreheads. They were told not to kill them but to torture them for five months with pain

like the pain of a scorpion sting. In those days people will seek death but will not find it. They will long to die, but death will flee from them!"(NLT).

Can you imagine the horror on the little children's faces as they see locusts stinging someone they love and hearing their screams of pain? The locusts may very well sting them as well if they are not disciples of our Lord Christ Jesus. This would be months of torture for those who are not disciples of Christ Jesus. How could our Lord Christ Jesus allow such a thing to happen? I am sure he would not. But, we are led to believe he would.

Revelation 9:7-11

"The locusts looked like horses prepared for battle. They had what looked like gold crowns on their heads, and their faces looked like human faces. They had hair like women's hair and teeth like the teeth of a lion. They wore armor made of iron, and their wings roared like an army of chariots rushing into battle. They had tails that stung like scorpions, and for five months they had the power to torment people. Their kind is the angel from the bottomless pit; his name in Hebrew is Abaddon, and in Greek, Apollyon-the Destroyer"(NLT).

Revelation 9:13-16

"Then the sixth angel blew his trumpet, and I heard a voice speaking from the four horns of the gold altar that stands in the presence of God. And the voice said to the sixth angel who held the trumpet, 'Release the four angels who are bound at the great Euphrates River.' Then the four angels who had prepared for this hour and day and month and year were turned loose to kill one-third of all the people on earth. I heard the size of their army, which was 200 million mounted troops"(NLT).

Revelation 9:17-19

"And in my vision, I saw the horses and the riders sitting on them. The riders wore armor that was fiery red and dark blue and yellow. The horses had heads like lions, and fire and smoke and burning sulfur billowed from their mouths. One-third of all the people on earth were killed by these three plagues-by the fire and smoke and burning sulfur that came from the mouths of the horses. Their power was in their mouths and in their tails. For their tails had heads like snakes, with the power to injure people"(NLT).

Revelation 9:20-21

"But the people who did not die in these plagues still refused to repent of their evil deeds and turn to God. They continued to worship demons and idols made of gold, silver, bronze, stone, and wood-idols that can neither see nor hear nor walk! And they did not repent of their murders or their witchcraft or their sexual immorality or their thefts"(NLT).

What John was describing appeared to be some future event he was seeing 1000 or 2000 years or more into the future, while living his life in the Middle East 2,000 years before. This made it was very hard for him to describe what he was seeing with great accuracy since it was so strange to him. This is why he referred to some things as looking like this or looking like that. Some of the descriptions we read of here may be mechanical devices of some kind. For instance, "The horses had heads like lions, and fire and smoke and burning sulfur billowed from their mouths. One-third of all the people on earth were killed by these three plagues-by the fire and smoke and burning sulfur that came from the mouths of the horses." Perhaps this description could be an engine of some sort that is burning gasoline and spewing out fire and smoke and burning sulfur. Also, the locusts described earlier might have been armored helicopters from the description given. Billowing smoke and dust being kicked up by their rotating blades.

Let Us Not Take the Book of Revelation to Seriously

After all, the Book of Revelation was intended to confuse and confound those who read it and Satan had his hand in inserting Scripture designed to confound and confuse the reader. Satan's efforts were intended to frighten us and cause us to fear our Lord God and make us believe our Lord God was causing all the destruction and fear and death and terrorizing billions of people, including little children. This is something that will help us to keep in context what John was trying to explain in the words he used during the time in which he lived. Not such an easy task; however, it was one he was asked to do, and overall, he did a remarkable job. How would you explain very high technology that seemed beyond description and that you had never laid eyes on before? Perhaps by comparing it to furious beasts. John would probably have never imagined that machines like those in the Book of Revelation could ever exist, yet he was told to write down and describe what he saw. This was what John did and this is why it is so hard to determine exactly what he is describing. It is sort of like the story of Ezekiel trying to describe the flying machine he saw one day which turned out to be pretty accurate. Aeronautical engineers were finally able to draw what Ezekiel described, and discovered some type of aerial machine that actually looked quite viable as an actual flying machine. And Ezekiel lived more than 2000 years ago. Anyway, this is the difficulty John faced and one which we face today as well as we try to figure out just what John was describing. This is why much of the Book of Revelation is so difficult to interpret to any reasonable degree and why we should not give too much credence to what we read in the Book of Revelation when it describes horrible events that are supposedly actions of our Lord God and His angels.

The Book of Revelation was never meant to be taken too seriously. Even John himself understood very little of Revelation and he often felt he should never have taken it to the Church's in Asia Minor. What I have just written concerning John came from our Lord Christ Jesus who is the one dictating this book and other information contained in it.

By the time John realized the Book of Revelation was probably not entirely from our Lord God, the damage had been done. John felt very bad concerning the writing of the Book of Revelation; however, he was way too old to be able to correct the harm done. John was about one-hundred and fifteen years old at the time he wrote the Book of Revelation. Do you believe that John, due to his advanced years, might have made a few mistakes in writing Revelation? This is why we should always take Revelation with a little bit of salt since Satan, who is the ruler of this world, works hard at corrupting the holy Words of our Lord God when given the opportunity to do so.

Discerning an Evil Number

For example, the Book of Revelation has many numbers within its pages that are not holy numbers. This; however, does not necessarily make them evil. Four examples are 2...4...7 and 8. The way you discern a holy number is, if it is a multiple of 3. Three is a holy number since it represents the Holy Trinity of our Lord God, our Lord Christ Jesus and The Holy Spirit. Christ Jesus died on the cross with his head at the 12 o'clock position, his left hand at the 3 o'clock position, his feet the 6 o'clock position and his right hand at the 9 o'clock position. Catholics make the symbol of the cross when they begin their prayers or give a blessing. Let me show you some examples of the importance of numbers in the holy Scriptures. Please read the following beginning first from Matthew all the way through Revelation. The parentheses at the beginning of each verse tells us how many instances a holy number has been used so far in all the verses up to that particular verse. The first verse below has a four placed just before the word Matthew, since there are four 'threes' used in that verse. The threes used are in red. Matthew 14:25 has one 'three' and so it has parentheses with '5', indicating there have, so far, been five 'threes' used in the first two verses included in this list. Continue reading each verse or verses given and you will see a trend emerge which may convince you of my theory concerning 'threes' and multiples of 'three'. I hope you enjoy reading and seeing these verses from a different light.

Counting the Number of 3s and 3rds in the New Testament

(4) MATTHEW: 12:40, "For as Jonah was in the belly of the great fish for three days and three nights, so will the Son of Man be in the heart of the earth for three days and three nights"(NLT).

(5) MATTHEW: 14:25, "About three o'clock in the morning Jesus came toward them, walking on the water"(NLT).

(6) MATTHEW: 15:32, "Then Jesus called his disciples and told them, 'I feel sorry for these people. They have been here with me for three days, and they have nothing left to eat'"(NLT).

(7) MATTHEW: 16:21, "He would be killed, but on the third day he would be raised from the dead"(NLT).

(8) MATTHEW: 17:4, "If you want, I'll make three shelters as memorials—one for you, one for Moses, and one for Elijah"(NLT).

(9) MATTHEW: 17:23, "He will be killed, but on the third day he will be raised from the dead"(NLT).

(10) MATTHEW 18:16, "But if you are unsuccessful, take one or two others with you and go back again, so that everything you say may be confirmed by two or three witnesses"(NLT).

(11) MATTHEW 20:5, "So they went to work in the vineyard. At noon and again at three o'clock he did the same thing"(NLT).

(12) MATTHEW 20:19, "But on the third day he will be raised from the dead"(NLT).

(13) MARK 8:31, "He would be killed, but three days later he would rise from the dead"(NLT).

(14) MARK 9:5, "Let's make three shelters as memorials—one for you, one for Moses, and one for Elijah"(NLT).

(15) MARK 9:31, "He will be killed, but three days later he will rise from the dead"(NLT).

(16) Mark 10:34, "They will mock him, spit on him, flog him with a whip, and kill him, but after three days he will rise again"(NLT).

(17) LUKE 1:56, "Mary stayed with Elizabeth about three months, and then went back to her own home"(NLT).

(18) LUKE 2:46, "Three days later they finally discovered him in the Temple, sitting among the religious teachers, listening to them and asking questions"(NLT).

(19) *LUKE 4:25, "Certainly there were many needy widows in Israel in Elijah's time, when the heavens were closed for* three *and a half years, and a severe famine devastated the land"(NLT).*

(20) *LUKE 9:22, "He will be killed, but on the* third *day he will be raised from the dead"(NLT).*

(21) *LUKE 10:36, "Now which of these* three *would you say was a neighbor to the man who was attacked by bandits?"(NLT).*

(22) *LUKE 11:5, "Suppose you went to a friend's house at midnight wanting to borrow* three *loaves of bread" (NLT).*

(24) *LUKE 12:52, "From now on families will be split apart,* three *in favor of me, and two against-or two in favor and* three *against"(NLT).*

(25) *LUKE 13:7, "Finally, he said to his gardener, 'I've waited for* three *years and there hasn't been a single fig!"(NLT).*

(26) *LUKE 13:21, "Even though she put only a little yeast in* three *measures of flour, it permeated every part of the dough"(NLT).*

(27) *LUKE 13:32, "Go tell that fox that I will keep on casting out demons and healing people today and tomorrow; and the* third *day I will accomplish my purpose"(NLT).*

(28) *LUKE 18:33, "They will flog him with a whip and kill him, but on the* third *day he will rise again"(NLT).*

(29) *LUKE 20:12, "A* third *man was sent, and they wounded him and chased him away"(NLT).*

(30) *LUKE 20:31, "Then the* third *brother married her"(NLT).*

(31) *LUKE* 22:61, "...Before the rooster crows tomorrow morning, you will deny *three* times that you even know me"(*NLT*).

(32) *LUKE* 23:22, "For the *third* time he demanded, "Why? What crime has he committed"(*NLT*).

(33) *LUKE* 23:44, "By this time is was about noon, and darkness fell across the whole land until *three* o'clock"(*NLT*).

(34) *LUKE* 24:6-7, "Remember what he told you back in Galilee, that the Son of Man must be betrayed into the hands of sinful men and be crucified, and that he would rise again on the *third* day"(*NLT*).

(35) *LUKE* 24:21, "We had hoped he was the Messiah who had come to rescue Israel. This all happened *three* days ago"(*NLT*).

(36) *LUKE* 24:46, "And he said, 'Yes, it was written long ago that the Messiah would suffer and die and rise from the dead on the *third* day'"(*NLT*).

(37) *JOHN* 2:19, "All right, 'Jesus replied.' Destroy this temple, and in *three* days I will raise it up"(*NLT*).

(38) *JOHN* 2:20, "What!" 'they exclaimed.' "It has taken forty-six years to build this Temple, and you can rebuild it in *three* days?"(*NLT*).

(39) John 6:19, "They had rowed *three* or four miles when suddenly they saw Jesus walking on the water toward the boat"(*NLT*).

(40) John 13:38, "Jesus answered, 'Die for me? I tell you the truth Peter-before the rooster crows tomorrow morning, you will deny *three* times that you even know me'"(*NLT*).

(41) JOHN 21:14, "This was the third time Jesus had appeared to his disciples since he had been raised from the dead"(NLT).

(43) John 21:17, "A third time he asked him, 'Simon son of John, do you love me?' Peter was hurt that Christ Jesus asked the question a third time."(NLT).

(44) Acts 3:1, "Peter and John went to the Temple one afternoon to take part in the three o'clock prayer service"(NLT).

(45) Acts 5:7, "About three hours later his wife came in, not knowing what had happened"(NLT).

(46) Acts 7:20, "At that time Moses was born-a beautiful child in God's eyes. His parents cared for him at home for three months"(NLT).

(47) Acts 9:9, "He remained there blind for three days and did not eat or drink"(NLT).

(48) Acts 10:3, "One afternoon about three o'clock, he had a vision in which he saw an angel of God coming toward him. 'Cornelius!' the angel said"(NLT).

(49) Acts 10:16, "The same vision was repeated three times. Then the sheet was suddenly pulled up to heaven"(NLT).

(50) Acts 10:30, "Cornelius replied, 'Four days ago I was praying in my house about this same time, three o'clock in the afternoon.'"(NLT).

(51) Acts 10:39-40, "They put him to death by hanging him on a cross, but God raised him to life on the third day"(NLT).

(52) Acts 19:8, "Then Paul went to the synagogue and preached boldly for the next three months, arguing persuasively about the Kingdom of God"(NLT).

(53) Acts 20:2-3, "Then he traveled down to Greece, where he stayed for three months"(NLT).

(54) Acts 20:9, "As Paul spoke on and on, a young man named Eutychus, sitting on the windowsill, became very drowsy. Finally, he fell sound asleep and dropped three stories to his death below"(NLT).

(55) Acts 20:31, "Watch out! Remember the three years I was with you-my constant watch and care over you night and day, and my many tears for you"(NLT).

(56) Acts 25:1-2, "Three days after Festus arrived in Caesarea to take over his new responsibilities, he left for Jerusalem, where the leading priests and other Jewish leaders met with him and made their accusations against Paul"(NLT).

(57) Acts 28:7, "Near the shore where we landed was an estate belonging to Publius, the chief official of the island. He welcomed us and treated us kindly for three days"(NLT).

(58) Acts 28:11, "It was three months after the shipwreck that we set sail on another ship that had wintered at the island—an Alexandrian ship with twin gods as its figurehead"(NLT).

(59) Acts 28:12, "Our first stop was Syracuse, where we stayed three days"(NLT).

(60) Acts 28:15, "Others joined us at The Three Taverns"(NLT).

(61) Acts 28:17, "Three days after Paul's arrival, he called together the local Jewish leaders"(NLT).

(62) 1st Corinthians 12:28, "Here are some of the parts God has appointed for the church: first are apostles, second are prophets, third are teachers, then those who do miracles, those who have the gift of healing, those who can help others, those who have the gift of leadership, those who speak in unknown languages"(NLT).

(63) 1st Corinthians 13:13, "Three things will last forever-faith, hope, and love-and the greatest of these is love"(NLT).

(64) 1st Corinthians 14:27, "No more than two or three should speak in tongues"(NLT).

(65) 1st Corinthians 14:29, "Let two or three people prophesy, and let the others evaluate what is said"(NLT).

(66) 1st Corinthians 15:4, "He was buried, and he was raised from the dead on the third day, just as the Scriptures said"(NLT).

(68) 2ⁿᵈ Corinthians 11:25, "Three times I was beaten with rods. Once I was stoned. Three times I was shipwrecked"(NLT).

(69) 2ⁿᵈ Corinthians 12:2, "I was caught up to the third heaven fourteen years ago"(NLT).

(70) 2ⁿᵈ Corinthians 12:8, "Three different times I begged the Lord to take it away"(NLT).

(71) 2ⁿᵈ Corinthians 12:14, "Now I am coming to you for the third time, and I will not be a burden to you"(NLT).

(73) 2nd Corinthians 13:1, "This is the third time I am coming to visit you (and as the Scriptures say, 'The facts of every case must be established by the testimony of two or three witnesses')"(NLT).

(74) Galatians 1:18, "Then three years later I went to Jerusalem to get to know Peter, and I stayed with him for fifteen days"(NLT).

(75) 1st Timothy 5:19, "Do not listen to an accusation against an elder unless it is confirmed by two or three witnesses"(NLT).

(76) Hebrews 10:28, "For anyone who refused to obey the law of Moses was put to death without mercy on the testimony of two or three witnesses"(NLT).

(77) Hebrews 11:23, "It was by faith that Moses' parents hid him for three months when he was born"(NLT).

(79) 1st John 5:7-8, "So we have these three witnesses-the Spirit, the water, and the blood-and all three agree"(NLT).

(81) Revelation 6:5, "When the Lamb broke the third seal, I heard the third living being say, 'Come!'" (NLT).

(82) Revelation 6:6, "And, I heard a voice from among the four living beings say, 'A loaf of wheat bread or three loaves of barley will cost a day's pay'"(NLT).

(83) Revelation 8:10, "Then the third angel blew his trumpet, and a great star fell from the sky, burning like a torch"(NLT).

(84) Revelation 8:13, "Then I looked, and I heard a single eagle crying loudly as it flew through the air, terror, terror, terror, to all who belong to this world because of what will happen when the last three angels blow their trumpets"(NLT).

(85) *Revelation 9:18, "One-third of all the people on earth were killed by these* three *plagues-by the fire and smoke and burning sulfur that came from the mouths of the horses"(NLT).*

(86) *Revelation 11:9, "And for* three *and a half days, all peoples, tribes, languages, and nations will stare at their bodies"(NLT).*

(87) *Revelation 11:11, "But after* three *and a half days, God breathed life into them, and they stood up!" (NLT).*

(88) *Revelation 11:14, "The second terror is past, but look, the* third *terror is coming quickly"(NLT).*

(89) *Revelation 16:4, "Then the* third *angel poured his bowl on the rivers and springs, and they became blood"(NLT).*

(90) *Revelation 16:13 "And I saw* three *evil spirits that looked like frogs leap from the mouths of the dragon, the beast and the false prophet"(NLT).*

(91) *Revelation 16:19 "The great city of Babylon split into* three *sections, and the cities of many nations fell into heaps of ruble"(NLT).*

(92) *Revelation 21:13 "There were* three *gates on each side-east, north, south and west"(NLT).*

(93) *Revelation 21:19, "The wall of the city was built on foundation stones inlaid with twelve precious stones: the first was jasper, the second sapphire, the* third *agate, the fourth emerald, the fifth onyx, the sixth carnelian, the seventh chrysolite, the eighth beryl, the ninth topaz, the tenth chrysoprase, the eleventh jacinth, the twelfth amethyst"(NLT).*

There is a total of 93 instances of three as you can see from the last parentheses with ninety-three inside, (93). If we add 9 + 3 the result is 12. Then, if we add 1 + 2 we have 3. This proves our Lord God's hand in the use of three's in the holy Scriptures.

[1] In regards to the Book of Ephesians, I found no three or third, or six, nor nine or twelve throughout Ephesians.

[2] In regards to the Book of Philippians, I found no three or third, or six, nor nine or twelve throughout Philippians.

[3] In regards to the Book of Colossians, I found no three or third, or six, nor nine or twelve throughout Colossians.

[4] In regards to the Book of 1st Thessalonians, I found no three or third, or six, nor nine or twelve throughout 1st Thessalonians.

[5] In regards to the Book of 2nd Thessalonians, I found no three or third, or six, nor nine or twelve throughout 2nd Thessalonians.

[6] In regards to the Book of 2nd Timothy, I found no three or third, or six, nor nine or twelve throughout 2nd Timothy.

[7] In regards to the Book of Titus, I found no three or third, or six, nor nine or twelve throughout Titus.

[8] In regards to the Book of Philemon, I found no three or third, or six, nor nine or twelve throughout Philemon.

[9] In regards to the Book of James, I found no three or third, or six, nor nine or twelve throughout James.

[10] In regards to the Book of 1st Peter, I found no three or third, or six, nor nine or twelve throughout 1st Peter.

[11] In regards to the Book of 2nd Peter, I found no three or third, or six, nor nine or twelve throughout 2nd Peter.

[12] In regards to the Book of 2nd John, I found no three or third, or six, nor nine or twelve throughout 2nd John.

[13] In regards to the Book of 3rd John, I found no three or third, or six, nor nine or twelve throughout 3rd John.

[14] In regards to the Book of Jude, I found no three or third, or six, nor nine or twelve throughout Jude.

It is interesting to note there are fourteen books in the New Testament which do not have a single three or third, nor six, or nine, or twelve, mentioned in them. However, I sure might have missed a few there. Perhaps you can find them.

As you can see, I found a total of 93 uses of the words three or third used in the New Testament holy Scripture. Some verses had the word 'third' which has the same meaning as three and I counted each of those to arrive at 93. Perhaps this is not all the 3s there are. If you should find more, please let me know. I will provide my business email at the end of this book in footnotes. Please keep in mind that you may find more three's or third's in the New Testament holy Scripture simply due to the fact they are not always easy to spot. There is a tendency to focus on what you are reading rather than looking for the words, three or third or six or nine or twelve. I suggest that you try reading the holy Scripture backward. This will help you to not focus on the meaning of the sentence you are currently reading. You can only be certain of finding all of the threes by reading every single book of the New Testament in your particular version and counting the number of times you come across three or third. Even if the verses repeat from one book of the New Testament to the next book of the New Testament. You must still count each time you come across a three or a third. For example, in the above verses I listed both Matthew 16:21 and Matthew 17:23. Both quotes are almost exactly the same. Both holy Scripture verses have third and should still be listed in your list of instances of three or third in order to come up with my count of 93.

What actually did happen to John during the time he wrote the Book of Revelation? He was imprisoned on the Island of Patmos. John was in prison for more than two years before he was finally released. Many people on the Island of Patmos petitioned that John be released since he had spent over two years in prison already. However, the local authorities continued to ignore their pleas. Our Lord God could have intervened at any time to free John; however, he did not. Would this not make you wonder if John could have held on to his faith for as long as he did? Apparently, John did hold strong to his faith since our Lord God entrusted him with the seven letters to the Church's in Asia and the Book of Revelation.

Did John speak with The Holy Spirit during his time of captivity? Yes, he certainly did. In fact, it was The Holy Spirit that was telling John most of what there was to know concerning the Book of Revelation. The reference to John speaking with The Holy Spirit is written in the holy Scripture at various places and it usually reads like this. "Anyone with ears to hear must listen to the Spirit and understand what he is saying to the Churches." Do you remember reading this phrase? It tells you everything you need to know concerning the fact it was The Holy Spirit that helped John write the seven letters to the Church's in Asia Minor.

The day finally came when John was allowed to leave his prison. The local Sadducee told John he was free to leave at any time. John got all of his gear together and walked out of prison a free man as long as he did not return to preaching the gospel. However, knowing John, that did not last very long and in due time John was back in prison. This went on for several years before enough people in the area became Christian and demanded of the local Sadducee judge to allow John to go free for good, since he had long ago served out his sentence. Under so much pressure, the local Sadducee judge agreed to release John for good no matter if he continued to preach the gospel or not. In the end John died at the ripe old age of 115 years of age. We know John's age approximately, since the Book of Revelation was dated as being written in 95 A.D. according to the New Living Translation of the holy Scriptures. John was probably about 20 years old when our Lord Christ Jesus selected him as one of his twelve disciples. Therefore, 95 plus 20 would make John roughly 115 years old or thereabouts when he wrote the Book of Revelation.

C H A P T E R   1 0

John Eats the Small Scroll

This chapter 10 once again contains several instances of 7, so I shall write those verses and discuss them as we read along. Here is the how the Book of Revelation chapter 10 begins.

Revelation 10:1-3
"Then I saw another mighty angel coming down from heaven, surrounded by a cloud, with a rainbow over his head. His face shone like the sun, and his feet were like pillars of fire. And in his hand was a small scroll that had been opened. He stood with his right foot on the sea and his left foot on the land. And he gave a great shout like the roar of a lion. And when he shouted, the seven thunders answered"(NLT).

Why would a mighty angel of our Lord God look like the one just described? Would all this extravagance be necessary if it were an angel of the Lord? No, since the angels of our Father in heaven are glorious beyond what is described here. They almost always wear brilliant white robes and their presence usually strikes fear in those who behold them and the one seeing the angel sense great power from them. Also, we see again the description of the angel's feet being like pillars of fire. We have seen this already in a description of our Lord Christ Jesus. Why would it be used twice to describe two different beings? Is it likely there is even fire in heaven? Think about that for a second or two. Try to imagine where in heaven we might see fire. Can we imagine heaven without fire? I can, quite easily.

Revelation 10:4

"When the seven thunders spoke, I was about to write. But I heard a voice from heaven saying, 'Keep secret what the seven thunders said, and do not write it down'"(NLT).

The Seven Thunders

Might the seven thunders be the voice of our Lord God? If so, why would it be necessary to block out his words? Why would the angel helping John ask him to block out the words of seven thunders? Perhaps it was not the Lord God who spoke those words since they referred to him at the seven thunders. Seven again is associated with Satan.

Revelation 10:5-7

"Then the angel I saw standing on the sea and on the land raised his right hand toward heaven. He swore an oath in the name of the one who lives forever and ever, who created the heavens and everything in them, the earth and everything in it, and the sea and everything in it. He said, 'There will be no more delay. When the seventh angel blows his trumpet, God's mysterious plan will be fulfilled. It will happen just as he announced it to his servants the prophets'"(NLT).

Would an oath be necessary in this case? It does not seem likely. The supposed angel from heaven swore an oath the seventh angel would blow his trumpet and then God's mysterious plan would be fulfilled. If our Lord God was behind this plan then it would happen without the need of an angel to swear to make it happen. Would it not make more sense for the angel from heaven to instead say, "I am here by the authority of our Lord God to see that the seventh angel blows his trumpet and carries out the mysterious plan of our Lord God." Does that phrase not seem more appropriate?

The remainder of this chapter deals with a small scroll that John was told to take and eat. John did eat it and it turned sour in his stomach just as the angel who gave it to him said it would. Then John was instructed to "...prophesy again about many people, nations, languages, and kings."

There is not much to this chapter 10 other than the one known as 'seven thunders.' Who might this person be. Perhaps it is our Lord God who has a booming voice when he speaks aloud, which he rarely does. Anyway, we are not told what the seven thunders said since John was told by an angel from heaven not to write the words of seven thunders down. Does this name not sound like the name of a native American? Seven Thunders!

The Two Prophets

In this chapter 11, we are told of two prophets who act more like two demons than prophets of our Lord God.

Revelation 11:4-6

"These two prophets are the two olive trees and the two lampstands that stand before the Lord of all of earth. If anyone tries to harm them, fire flashes from their mouths and consumes their enemies. This is how anyone who tries to harm them must die. They have power to shut the sky so that no rain will fall for as long as they prophesy. And they have the power to turn the rivers and oceans into blood, and to strike the earth with every kind of plague as often as they wish."

The Two Prophets

These two prophets will prophesy for 1260 days which is 42 weeks. Now, let us ask this question. Who exactly is Lord of all the Earth? Lord of all the Earth is not something you hear spoken of much. Is it our Lord God in heaven? Or is it Satan? According to our Lord Christ Jesus speaking in

John 12:31, Satan is the ruler of this world and according to Paul in 2nd Corinthians 4:4, Satan is the god of this world. Could Revelation 11:14 actually be speaking of Satan as the Lord of all the Earth? Perhaps you might believe so after you read what is to come.

Just who were the two prophets spoken of in the above verses? Could they be our Lord God's prophets? It does not seem likely after one investigates their actions. Does it not seem odd these alleged prophets had the power to cause plagues any time they decided to do so? Would our Lord God choose to send two evil prophets to alert His people to the fact they were in grave danger from Satan? Perhaps, though it would seem very unlikely. These two prophets would be more acceptable to our Lord God's children if they were to deliver a message of hope and salvation. However, it seems this is not what they were doing. We do not know what message they were delivering to the people of Earth since we are not told. Although we do know they were spreading fear and terror. So, what exactly were these two prophets up to.

Let us look at all the horror they bring to the world. Turning rivers and oceans into blood. Burning people alive who may oppose their message with flames of fire from their mouth. Does this sound like any prophet our Lord God ever sent to Earth to witness and prophecy? Is it any wonder why the people were so fearful of these two alleged prophets who spread fear and death wherever they went? Could it be they were working for Satan instead, and were not actually prophets from our Lord God? This is a distinct possibility. Our Lord God has always sent prophets to spread His Word who were always speaking to the people of love and kindness toward one another and not murder and mayhem. Who else might these two prophets represent other than Satan? Who rushes in to declare war against these two prophets? This is stated next.

Revelation 11:7

"When they complete their testimony, the beast that comes up out of the bottomless pit will declare war against them, and he will conquer and kill them."

Satan Declares War on the Two Prophets

It is Satan who declares war on these two prophets. Is it likely that Satan could attack and destroy two of our Lord God's prophets? Unfortunately, yes, since it happened to many of the prophets our Lord God sent to His children to warn them away from the direction they were then going.

Why would Satan declare war on the two prophets who were terrorizing the people of Earth? Might Satan be trying to appear as a good deity to fool the people into believing they should turn away from our Lord God and instead follow him? After all, it was the beast from the bottomless pit who destroyed the two prophets who were spreading disaster and horrors wherever they went.

If we were living during the end-of-times and if everyone expected our Lord God to take out His wraith upon the people of Earth during the last days, does it not make sense that the people of Earth would believe our Lord God was behind the horrors which would be happening during the last days? And, would not Satan enjoy convincing the people of Earth he was really their savior and not our Lord God? And, our Lord God was very frightening and filled us with terror. Perhaps this is why the two evil prophets were sent; to make it appear they were sent by our Lord God, when in reality they were evil spirits sent by Satan himself. Our Lord God would never torment His children, since torture, torment, and death are in Satan's realm. Instead, our Lord God would send a prophet to warn the people where they were going wrong and try to help them change their ways. Our Lord God loves His earthly children more than you could possibly love your own children. This is why we should always question the holy Scripture that describes our Lord God as a God of mass murder, mass torture, or a purveyor of pain. Our Lord God is not that way at all. He is a loving, compassionate, kind, forgiving, patient, merciful, just, wise, and graceful Lord God as described by our Lord Christ Jesus. This chapter 11 describes evil events happening to people who suffered greatly from two alleged profits who spread terror and destructive events, supposedly, in the name of our Father in heaven. This is one more chapter in the Book of Revelation tainted by Satan himself.

CHAPTER 12

The Woman and the Beast

Then John saw a woman in heaven dressed with the sun and the moon was near her feet. There were twelve stars just above her head. She was with child and in labor due to the agony of giving birth. Just as she appeared in the heavens, a Lion was seen with the planet Jupiter and the star Regulus near each other. Jupiter is called the king planet since ancient times and Regulus is known as the king star. As you know, the tribe of Judah has the Lion as its symbol and the Lion is called the king of the jungle. So, we see three symbols for king; the Lion, Jupiter, and Regulus. What might this mean and why was John seeing this in the heavens?

The Red Dragon

Then John saw another event in heaven with great significance. John saw a large red dragon with seven heads and ten horns with seven crowns on its heads. Each head had its own crown. Could this possibly be related to what we have covered before when the beast was described with seven heads and ten crowns on each of the seven heads? Perhaps so. It does look like more than coincidence. Continuing, the red dragon swept away one-third of the stars from heaven and threw them to Earth. What could this mean? I remember reading that when a star falls to Earth it usually means an angel of the Lord is descending to Earth with a message for one of his prophets. However, when one-third of the stars in heaven are thrown to Earth it must be one very big event. We will discuss this more later.

After this, John saw the woman give birth to a child who was to rule all nations with an iron rod. Her child was snatched away to heaven where the red dragon could not reach him. One day soon he would return to claim all of those who were his followers. However, in the meantime, his mother would have to hide away for 1260 days in a far-off land known as Ethiopia. A land south along the Nile River where she stayed until the danger of persecution had passed. Then she returned to Israel and journeyed back to her home and reunited with old friends and family. She would live out the rest of her life in virtual obscurity. No one seemed to care she was the mother of our Lord Christ Jesus. She raised no more children since her husband Joseph died even while she was still quite young. What I have just written here was dictated to me by our Lord Christ Jesus.

Revelation 12:7-9

"Then there was war in heaven. Michael and his angels fought against the dragon and his angels. And the dragon lost the battle, and he and his angels were forced out of heaven. This great dragon - the ancient serpent called the devil, or Satan, the one deceiving the whole world -was thrown down to earth with his angels"(NLT).

The Final Battle in Heaven

The above holy Scripture may actually be written in the stars and constellations. I will attempt to interpret the above holy Scripture in the constellations of the Zodiac with the help of Mr. Larson, whom you will hear more of later in this chapter. I believe you will find it most interesting. For instance, the Constellation of Scorpio is the constellation which shows the great dragon sweeping one-third of the stars of heaven to Earth with its sweeping scorpion tail. It is this constellation which grabs hold of the cross in the Constellation of Libra which represents the baby Jesus, in hopes of devouring baby Jesus soon after he is born on Earth. However, this never happened since our Lord God quickly took our Lord Christ Jesus home with Him in heaven. From the time that baby Jesus was born on Earth until the time he was crucified on the cross at Golgotha till he was taken home to be with his Father in heaven was all recorded in the constellations. This time span represents only a small fraction of time for our Lord God to provide protection for Christ Jesus on Earth. This may seem a long time for those of us living on Earth; however, it is but a twinkling of an eye in our Lord God's scale of time.

The Star of Bethlehem

After reading the paragraphs above I believe we can see there are messages written in the constellations. Let me give you some helpful information where you can watch a presentation called "The Star of Bethlehem" by Rick Larson. You can find it on YouTube or go to the website set up by Rick Larson at www.bethlehemstar.com. What is to be witnessed in his video presentation will be amazing and perhaps life changing for some. Mr. Larson begins by explaining the stars hold hidden messages for us to view and interpret. Mr. Larson uses biblical references to show this. Mr. Larson will explain his findings and research which will challenge some of what we may have believed in regards to the Star of Bethlehem. Mr. Larson will show you with astronomical software the actual Star of Bethlehem during the very time when our Lord Christ Jesus was about to be born. It is the actual star. The astronomy software Mr. Larson has, has the ability to take us back to anytime in the distant past we might like to view and show us in great accuracy and detail the constellations, planets, and stars at that very moment in time in history and their positions in the sky. This can be done with the twelve constellations as well, as you will see in Mr. Larson's presentation video. I will not tell of all the amazing discoveries he made since that would spoil the whole presentation for you. I am sure you will find it quite amazing, as I did. However, I can say there are two constellations mentioned in Mr. Larson's presentation. Those two being the Constellation of Leo the Lion which represents the tribe of Judah, and our Lord Christ Jesus, and the Constellation of Virgo which represents the Virgin Mary.

During Mr. Larson's presentation of The Star of Bethlehem, the Constellation of Libra and the Constellation of Scorpio were not mentioned in Mr. Larson's presentation. I believe this was due to Mr. Larson not being aware of the significance of these two nearby constellations to his presentation.

It should be mentioned the Constellation of Scorpio was changed by the Roman Emperor Ptolemy in the 2nd Century. Before Emperor Ptolemy made his change, the Constellation of Libra was part of the Constellation of Scorpio which existed during the time Christ Jesus walked the Earth. Ptolemy created Libra from Scorpio in the 2nd century. Almost 200 years after Christ Jesus walked the Earth. Thus, Ptolemy gave us the Constellation of Libra that we know today. Libra came to represent the scales of

justice or balance. Today, the Constellation of Scorpio no longer looks like a huge scorpion grabbing hold of the Constellation of Libra. Its two pincers have been severed from its arms. You will find the source of my information in the hyperlink just below.
Source: Constellation Guide - Constellations: A Guide to the Night Sky. The website address is: http://www.constellation-guide.com/constellation-list/libra-constellation/, 2022.

Let us now have a look at the Constellation of Libra. If you look closely at Libra, you will see four distinct stars which form a lopsided cross. Long ago when Libra was still part of the Constellation of Scorpio it was recognized that two of the claws of Scorpio were holding on to this cross. One claw at the top and one claw at the bottom of Libra. The Sumerians called the Constellation of Scorpio, Gir-Tab which means "the Scorpion" about 5,000 years ago. Even the Egyptian Temple at Denderah shows the Constellation of Scorpio on its walls. Below is some additional evidence describing which stars represented the claws of Scorpio.

"As a reminder, Libra was once considered a part of Scorpio constellation, the brightest star in Libra, Beta Librae, has the name Zubeneschamali, which means 'the northern claw' in Arabic, while another star, Alpha Librae, Zubenelgenubi, is 'the southern claw.'"

"Ancient Greeks knew the part of the sky occupied by the Constellation of Libra as Chelae, or "claws," and considered it part of the Scorpio constellation. Chelae represented the scorpion's claws."

(Source: Constellation Guide, Constellations: A Guide to the Night Sky. https://www.constellation-guide.com/constellation-list/libra-constellation/,2022)

"Scorpius dates back to when the Zodiac consisted of only six constellations."
(Source: Pedigree Books, 1984, "Star Watch" by Ben Mayer, A.R.C.A.)

The Constellations in the Night Sky

Now, let us look to the Constellation of Virgo which is also known as the Virgin and represents mother Mary who is our Lord Christ Jesus' mother. Mr. Larson explains the role of the Constellation of Virgo excellently in his presentation. Mr. Larson's presentation misses a few details since he did not speak of the Constellation of Libra or the Constellation of Scorpio. I would like to add what I believe Mr. Larson missed since I am sure it will add to your experience and enjoyment of Mr. Larson's story line concerning The Star of Bethlehem. Mr. Larson, as mentioned before, leaves out the Constellations of Libra and Scorpio both of which play an important role in the explanation of our Lord Christ Jesus' early life as displayed in the heavens, as I will attempt to show.

If you know how to locate the constellations in the night sky, then you are probably familiar with how they move across the sky from east to west. Mr. Larson first covers the Constellation of Leo, which represents a Lion and was the symbol of Judah where our Lord Christ Jesus was born. The Constellation of Leo comes before the Constellation of Virgo as if to announce the beginning of our Lord Christ Jesus birth and death to come.

Immediately following the Constellation of Leo is the Constellation of Virgo which represents mother Mary, Christ Jesus' mother. Below is how the coming of our Lord Christ Jesus was revealed in the stars.

Revelation 12:1-2
"Then I witnessed in heaven an event of great significance. I saw a woman clothed with the sun, with the moon beneath her feet, and a crown of twelve stars on her head. She was pregnant, and she cried out because of her labor pains and the agony of giving birth"(NLT).

Mr. Larson's presentation will actually show the exact time and date when the above event took place. You will see the moon at the foot of the Constellation of Virgo as it rises into the sky with the sun shining brightly in Virgo dramatizing that mother Mary was clothed with the sun. Mr. Larson explains the role of the Constellation of Virgo very well in his presentation.

For those who have seen Mr. Larson's presentation of the "Star of Bethlehem" then you know the above verse is speaking of the Constellation of Virgo on a certain date. In Virgo we find the announced birth of our Lord Christ Jesus himself and it was written there in the stars of the Constellation of Virgo more than 5000 years before the birth of Christ Jesus. And, to be correct, the Constellation of Virgo may have been there since the beginning of creation. Satan could see this constellation as well, so Satan knew the approximate date the Messiah would be born on Earth. It was our Lord God's desire that Satan not know the exact specifics of our Lord Christ Jesus' birth. And, to be correct, the Constellation of Virgo may have been there since the beginning of creation.

The Constellation of Libra follows immediately after the Constellation of Virgo has risen high into the sky. Just to remind you, the Constellation of Libra has a lopsided cross with four main stars making up the cross. If you look at the modern interpretation of Libra, it shows a not well-defined triangle. If we look at the four main stars that make up Libra, we will see they form a cross which was known during the time our Lord Christ Jesus was on Earth.

Next in line of the constellations of the Zodiac is the Constellation of Scorpio. Scorpio is the constellation associated with Satan and for good reason. It is a very large scorpion with two large pincers that are reaching for the Constellation of Libra and is holding the top of the cross and the bottom of the cross ready to devour baby Jesus even as he is born. The cross represents baby Jesus. The Book of Revelation speaks of a large red dragon that sweeps up one-third of the stars of heaven and casts them to Earth. For those of us who may not know, Satan and the angels who were his followers were all cast to Earth since no room could be found for them in heaven after they revolted. This was covered in Revelation 12:7-9. Here is how it reads.

Revelation 12:7-9

"Then there was war in heaven. Michael and his angels fought against the dragon and his angels. And the dragon lost the battle, and he and his angels were forced out of heaven. This great dragon-the ancient serpent called the devil, or Satan, the one deceiving the whole world-was thrown down to the earth with all his angels"(NLT).

Our Lord God's Angels are Deceived

The stars swept from the heavens mentioned in the Book of Revelation 12:3-4 represent the fallen angels who were followers of Satan although they were deceived into following him. All of the angels in heaven who became followers of Satan were very innocent in the ways of evil. They did not know what evil meant or what it was. They did not know what a lie was. When Satan convinced the angels in heaven they could be just like our Lord God if they knew and understood what evil was, they naturally believed Satan since they had never heard a lie and did not know what a lie was.

Notice that evil spelled backward is live. To know evil is to know death.

Our Lord Christ Jesus mentioned several times during his ministry those of us here on Earth were dead. Perhaps what he meant by that is our lives on Earth are so bad compared to the angels in heaven we were like the living dead. If we could compare our lives to those of the angels in heaven then we would realize our lives are lifeless and unfulfilled compared to the angels in heaven.

This concludes the presentation of all the constellations that demonstrate the birth of our Lord Christ Jesus, mother Mary, the cross, and Satan's attempt to end our Lord Christ Jesus mission, which was to save all the people on Earth from Satan. Of course, the Constellation of Leo began the precession of the four constellations in our presentation. There was more to the Constellation of Leo than you might know; however, it was too time consuming to go through ever little detail. In Mr. Larson's presentation of "The Star of Bethlehem" he shows in detail the crowning of Jupiter three times. Jupiter is known as the king of all the planets. Leo the Lion, was the symbol for Judah and the lion was the king of the animal kingdom, and the star of Rigel which in ancient times was known as the king star. All three of these make a near alignment in Leo just before the birth of our Lord Christ Jesus. You will this clearly in Mr. Larson's presentation. Does this not clearly demonstrate that an important event was about to happen? I certainly believe it does.

So, there you have it. This explains why all of us are living on Earth with the presence of Satan all around us every day of our lives. It also explains why our lives are filled with disasters and personal loss. Why wars exist and why we rarely have peace and consistent prosperity. Why there is always a struggle for freedom against those who would enslave us. It also explains why our Lord Christ Jesus came to Earth, to rescue us from Satan and make it possible for all of our sins to be forgiven so that we can once again return home to our Father in heaven.

There is one more verse that is also telling of our existence on Earth and it too is in the Book of Revelation, chapter 12. This verse reads as follows.

Revelation 12:17

"And the dragon was angry with the woman and declared war against the rest of her children-all who keep God's commandments and maintain their testimony for Jesus"(NLT).

The Red Dragon is Angry with Mother Mary

The woman mentioned in the above verse is none other than mother Mary, our Lord Christ Jesus' mother. Is this not a very telling verse? It is made abundantly clear in the above verse that all who are disciples of our Lord Christ Jesus are considered enemies of Satan and he hopes to destroy every one of those who are disciples of our Lord Christ Jesus and who keep his commandments and maintain their testimony of Jesus. Can Satan do that? Yes, he can if we stray too far from our Lord God's protection. If a sheep from a sheep herders flock strays too far a hungry wolf can snatch up that stray sheep and make away with it before it is even missed. It is the same with our Lord God. If we stray too far from our Lord God then we too can be snatched up by a roaring Lion like Satan. So, be sure to stay close to our Lord God by praying daily for His protection and by reading the holy Scripture to keep yourself alert to Satan's deceptions. Satan will do all he can to lure you away from the protection of our Lord God, so be alert to Satan's lies and deceptions. Christ Jesus told his disciples that Satan is the father of lies, and so it is written.

CHAPTER 13

The Beast Out of the Sea,
The Beast Out of the Earth

n the very first verse in chapter 13 we find yet another 7. Here is how that holy Scripture reads.

Revelation 13:1-2
"Then I saw a beast rising up out of the sea. It had seven heads and ten horns, with ten crowns on its horns. And written on each head were names that blasphemed God. This beast looked like a leopard, but it had the feet of a bear and the mouth of a lion! And the dragon gave the beast his own power and throne and great authority"(NLT).

Does the above verse sound familiar to you? It should. We read in chapter 12 a similar verse. Here is that verse from chapter 12.

Revelation 12:3-4
"Then I witnessed in heaven another significant event. I saw a large red dragon with seven heads and ten horns, with seven crowns on his heads. His tail swept away one-third of the stars

71

in the sky, and he threw them to the earth. He stood in front of the woman as she was about to give birth, ready to devour her baby as soon as it was born"(NLT).

This certainly indicates that the beast with seven heads and ten horns, with seven crowns on his heads is most certainly Satan. The only difference is that the beast rising from the sea had ten crowns of his head. Anyway, let us continue.

As from previous chapters, when we see 7 in the beginning of Scripture we should not take it seriously. How could we when it describes a beast that looked like a leopard with the feet of a bear and the mouth of a lion. What are we supposed to make of that? Also, it had 7 heads and 10 horns with 10 crowns on each head. It is likely that the heads and horns represent people and perhaps people with the power of kings. There were 10 crowns on each of the 7 heads, so 70 crowns in total. Perhaps it represented all the kings on Earth at one time. Kings still exist even now. Also, in this chapter 13 verses 5-8 tells a very strange story. Almost as if it were taken from a very ancient text.

Revelation 13:5-8

"Then the beast was allowed to speak great blasphemies against God. And he was given authority to do whatever he wanted for forty-two months. And he spoke terrible words of blasphemy against God, slandering his name and his dwelling-that is, those who dwell in heaven. And the beast was allowed to wage war against God's holy people and to conquer them. And he was given authority to rule over every tribe and people and language and nation. And all the people who belong to this world worshiped the beast. They are the ones whose names were not written in the Book of Life that belongs to the Lamb who was slaughtered before the world was made"(NLT).

A Very Ancient Story

What can we make of this holy Scripture? It seems as if it was written many eons of time ago. Far beyond our present time. I say this since it tells us the Lamb was slaughtered before the world was made. How can that be? How could our Lord Christ Jesus have been slaughtered before the world was made? Perhaps it refers to a time or age long before the present age, with an age being approximately 2,000 years long. There were no people on Earth for tens of millions of years before it finally became a habitable planet. For many millions of years Earth's atmosphere was toxic and no life could exist. It took many more millions of years for the first signs of life to show themselves. So, how is it possible our Lord Christ Jesus was sacrificed before the world was made? Perhaps the writers were writing of a time when there were people on the Earth who were all followers of Satan.

The time period before the present time period was much worse than it presently is. It is shown that about 10,000 to 12,000 years ago a great disaster swept the world and leveled many then existing civilizations. Some of these civilizations were swept away by a giant flood. Geologist Randall Carson speaks of a great flood that inundated much of the western U.S. about 11,600 years ago. It destroyed many people living in the America's during that time and much of the fauna as well. The Wooly Mammoth, the American Pigmy Horse, the Giant Ground Sloth, the Sabre Tooth Tiger, a Lion that was as large as a present-day horse and many other species that no longer exist. Some species of humans were also swept away in the great flood and no longer exist. Some, of the remains of these civilizations are only now being unearthed.

Ancient Gobekli Tepe

Gobekli Tepe is one such example dating back to more than 11,600 years ago. It was a highly advanced race of people who were not only hunter gathers, but also cultivated crops and domesticated animals. Only 10 percent of Gobekli Tepe has so far been excavated. Ninety percent still remains to be unearthed. Who could have created such a civilization? Were they the survivors of the Great Flood spoken of in the Old Testament, or the victims of that flood? Gobekli Tepe is not very far from Mount Ararat in Turkey. Perhaps the recent earthquake in Southern Turkey and Northern Syria will reveal more of this long extinct civilization. Abraham was born not far from Gobekli Tepe himself in the city of Sanliurfa, also known as Urfa in present day southern Turkey. Please notice that Urfa is the last four letters in Sanliurfa. This is quite interesting, all the fascinating coincidences surrounding Gobekli Tepe. Such as Abraham's birth place being located nearby and Mount Ararat also near to Gobekli Tepe as well. Hopefully, we will soon hear of more fantastic discoveries in this part of the world. But, what about our Lord Christ Jesus being slaughtered before the world began. Could it be that the ancient people did not realize there was another civilization before their own? According to Genesis, only a very few people survived that flood and they may not have kept proper records, or perhaps they were instructed to forget the previous civilization ever existed. So, it is possible that Christ Jesus came to this world before on very much the same mission, to save humankind from Satan who has destroyed human civilizations many times and is close to destroying yet another great civilization.

Also mentioned in this chapter is the number 666. The mark of the beast is the number 666, according to the holy Scriptures and is the number of a man. However, what number might this be? Could it be part of their social security number, or a credit card number, or perhaps a brand on their body from being in prison. Prisoners often brand themselves with a hot iron to show their manhood and bravery. This number could be derived from any number of things.

Notice that the number 666 adds up to, 6 + 6 + 6 = 18. And, 18 adds to up, 1 + 8 = 9. The number 9 is a holy number, so could this mean we are being misled concerning the number 666? Perhaps it is not the mark of the beast after all.

We do know 7, is a symbol for Satan? Due to the fact that Satan has 7 aspects and they are once again; pride, envy, avarice, anger, luxury, intemperance, and sloth. These are the 7 worst sins, which lead to all other sins. They represent the 7 crowns which the beast wears. The 10 horns were the triumphs of the iniquity and malice of the dragon and the vain and arrogant glorification and exaltation which he attributed to himself in the execution of his wickedness. I would refer you to the Book of Revelation 12:3-4, which is very near the beginning of this chapter.

The Great Persecution Following our Lord Christ Jesus' Death

A great persecution of Christians followed soon after our Lord Christ Jesus died at Golgotha on the cross. Our Lord Christ Jesus told me this when I was being attacked by Satan and his demons. I wrote of my experience in "Satan's World." That is why I speak as if I know some of what happened during this period of time.

Let us now get back to where we were. According to Christ Jesus, mother Mary was forced to flee from the dragon, Satan, who was lord of Earth. She and her entourage, which included Mary Magdalene took a ship down the Nile River to the nation of Ethiopia. Here, mother Mary remained for 1260 days. This you will find in Revelation 12:6. Here below is a short piece of Scripture that may shed some light.

Revelation 12:15-17

"Then the dragon tried to drown the woman with a flood of water that flowed from his mouth. But the earth helped her by opening its mouth and swallowing the river that gushed out from the mouth of the dragon. And the dragon was angry at the woman and declared war against the rest of her children-all who keep God's commandments and maintain their testimony for Jesus"(NLT).

By the way, 1260 adds up to 9 as well. 1 + 2 + 6 + 0 = 9. Also, only after 1260 days had passed did mother Mary dare to return to her family in Israel. Twelve hundred and sixty days is approximately 42 months. During her time in Ethiopia mother Mary tried hard to keep a low profile and not get noticed. Even in Ethiopia, mother Mary was not completely safe. As she stayed there with her servants as the days went by very slowly.

From what we have just seen in the verses of the holy Scripture in this chapter 13 and other chapters as well, each demonstrate that the number 7 is not a holy number since it represents Satan and the 7 different aspects of Satan. Therefore, we should try to avoid taking seriously these verses in the Book of Revelation, which, from the beginning, give us the number 7 to consider.

CHAPTER 14

144,000 Virgin Men

In this chapter 14 there is the situation of the 144,000 virgin men who are to be gifted to our Lord Christ Jesus. They were purchased for our Lord Christ Jesus. How someone could purchase 144,000 virgin men remains a mystery. What significance would 144,000 virgin men be? Surely, the only one who could purchase these virgin men would be none other than our Lord Christ Jesus when he died on the cross and purchased them with his blood. However, you do not have to be a virgin for our Lord Christ Jesus to purchase you with his blood. Anyway, this is a little strange when you think about it. The part of the holy Scripture that speaks of these virgin men reads as follows.

Revelation 14:4-5
"They have been purchased from among the people on the earth as a special offering to God and to the Lamb. They have told no lies; they are without blame"(NLT).

Now, how could these 144,000 men, who were virgins and who have told no lives, be so perfect? It does not seem likely, does it? And, what about women? Why were no virgin women purchased as a special offering for our Lord God and our Lord Christ Jesus? This illustrates that women were not held in high regard by the Jewish people during that time. When our Lord Christ Jesus feed the 4,000 thousand and later the 5,000, the men were counted and later the holy Scripture would read, 'along with the women and children who were also present that day,' as if men were far more important than women and children. Also, in the chapter 14, are three angels seen flying through the sky. The first angel gave this message to the people of Earth.

Revelation 14:7
"Fear God," he shouted. "Give glory to him. For the time has come when he will sit as judge. Worship him who made the heavens, the earth, the sea, and all the springs of water"(NLT).

The second angel then followed with the next message to the people of Earth.

Revelation 14:8
"Babylon has fallen-that great city is fallen-because she made all the nations of the world drink the wine of her passionate immorality"(NLT).

Then the third angel spoke and said the following to all the people of Earth.

Revelation 14:9-11
"Anyone who worships the beast and his statue or who accepts his mark on the forehead or on the hand must drink the wine of God's anger. It has been poured full strength into God's cup of wrath. And they will be tormented with fire and burning sulfur in the presence of the holy angels and the Lamb. The smoke of their torment will rise forever and ever, and they will have no

relief day or night, for they have worshiped the beast and his statue and have accepted the mark of his name"(NLT).

Our Lord Christ Jesus Would Never Enjoy the Suffering of Others

Based upon the verses just above where it states, "they will be tormented with fire and burning sulfur in the presence of the holy angels and the Lamb," we can be sure of this, our Lord Christ Jesus would never go to hell to watch people burn as if to enjoy their torment. And, never would our Lord Christ Jesus ask our Father's innocent angels from heaven to watch people burning in agony. This would be an extremely sadistic act and only Satan himself or his demons could enjoy watching such a display of human suffering. Knowing this, should be take these holy Scripture verses seriously? They seem to want to make us believe badly of our Lord Christ Jesus and his Father's holy angels. This is something we have seen through much of Revelation where angels were given the task of spreading pain and misery upon the people of Earth. Who might want us to believe that our Lord Christ Jesus and angels from heaven would be so cruel and heartless? Perhaps Satan?

What Follows Next is a Description of the Rapture

Revelation 14:14
"Then I saw a white cloud, and seated on the cloud was someone like the Son of Man. He had a gold crown on his head and a sharp sickle in his hand"(NLT).

Is it not interesting that we keep seeing written "like the Son of Man." Never does it read, "the Son of Man." Could this mean John was not sure who was actually sitting on the cloud? Maybe John saw a figure sitting there but was uncertain if it was our Lord Christ Jesus. Why else would John say, "like the Son of Man." If I were to say to someone, it looks like John the Apostle; however, I could not be sure it was John the Apostle; still, it looked like John the Apostle. Could this be why John is describing the man sitting on the cloud as looking "like the Son of Man." Because John was not sure. Why not state emphatically, "it was the Son of Man?" Who might be sitting on that cloud?

Revelation 14:15-16
"Then another angel came from the Temple and shouted to the one sitting on the cloud, 'Swing the sickle, for the time of the harvest has come; the crop on earth is ripe.' So the one sitting on the cloud swung his sickle over the earth, and the whole earth was harvested"(NLT).

In the above verse where it reads, "So the one sitting on the cloud swung his sickle over the earth, and the whole earth was harvested." Why did it not describe the one sitting on the cloud as our Lord Christ Jesus instead of, "the one sitting on the cloud?" After all, he is the one who will rapture every true Christian from the tribulations then occurring and take them to heaven.

Might the man sitting on the cloud, who was given an order by another angel to now harvest the people of earth, for they are ripe for harvesting,' be another angel? Why would an angel be commanding our Lord Christ Jesus to swing his sickle? Our Lord Christ Jesus is part of the Trinity of our Lord God and created all of creation for our Father in heaven. Should we not expect Christ Jesus to know when the time has come to harvest the Christians of Earth? I believe we should.

Revelation 14:17-20

"After that, another angel came from the Temple in heaven, and he also had a sharp sickle. Then another angel, who had power to destroy with fire, came from the altar. He shouted to the angel with the sharp sickle, 'Swing your sickle now to gather the clusters of grapes from the vines of the earth, for they are ripe for judgment.' So the angel swung his sickle over the earth and loaded the grapes into the great winepress of God's wrath. The grapes were trampled in the winepress outside the city, and blood flowed from the winepress in a stream about 180 miles long and as high as a horse's bridle"(NLT).

If this were an angel of the Lord describing the actual rapture would it not have been more instructive to actually describe the rapture in real terms instead of using the symbolism employed in this chapter? If you want to read a better description of the rapture I have added it just below.

Matthew 24:29-31

"Immediately after the anguish of those days, the sun will be darkened, the moon will give no light, the stars will fall from the sky, and the powers in the heavens will be shaken.

"And then at last, the sign that the Son of Man is coming will appear in the heavens, and there will be deep morning among all the peoples on the earth. And they will see the Son of Man coming on the clouds of heaven with power and great glory. And he will send out his angels with the mighty blast of a trumpet, and they will gather his chosen ones from all over the world-from the farthest ends of the earth and heaven"(NLT).

Instead of a sickle would it not have been more descriptive to describe the people of Earth who were true Christians being taken up to heaven by angels who would escort them to heaven? So, perhaps what we are reading in

Revelation 14:17-20 is not written by our Lord God after all. For instance, the idea our Lord God would have the disciples of Satan, those who were not true Christians, being trampled alive in a giant winepress and then describing the amount of blood flowing from the winepress as long as 180 miles long and as high as a horse's bridle, a little too grotesque? Who or what is going to trample all of these billions of people before they are then thrown in the fiery pits of burning sulfur? Usually, it is people who trample the grapes in a winepress. This seems far beyond believable. Anyway, thus ends chapter 14.

CHAPTER 15

Completion of God's Wrath

In this chapter 15, the seven angels pour out seven last plagues, allegedly because our Father in heaven is very angry with His children and He decides to punish them with seven plagues.

Revelation 15:1

"Then I saw in heaven another marvelous event of great significance. Seven angels were holding the seven last plagues, which would bring God's wrath to completion"(NLT).

Can we believe that John was actually looking forward to seeing the last seven plagues unleashed upon the Earth? After all it does read "Then I saw in heaven another marvelous event of great significance." What is so marvelous about the seven last plagues? Perhaps if you were Satan you would look forward to watching the deaths and sufferings of billions of people worldwide. But, not John.

As was explained before, whenever the number 7 appears in a chapter in the Book of Revelation it is very likely that chapter has been corrupted by Satan. Later on, in this chapter there is also mentioned 7 bowls with the 7 last plagues. More evidence that Satan has corrupted this chapter as well. Almost always when 7 comes up it means mass death and destruction and incredible creatures beyond anyone's imagining. Being perhaps crafted by Satan to affect our imagination in horrible ways.

Revelation 15:5-8

"Then I looked and saw that the Temple in heaven, God's Tabernacle, was thrown wide open. The seven angels who were holding the seven last plagues came out of the Temple. They were clothed in spotless white linen with gold sashes across their chests. Then one of the four living beings handed each of the seven angels a gold bowl filled with the wrath of God, who lives forever and ever. The Temple was filled with smoke from God's glory and power. No one could enter the Temple until the seven angels had completed pouring out the seven plagues"(NLT).

Nothing in this chapter makes much sense. For instance, our Lord God's Temple in heaven being filled with smoke. Does this not give you pause to imagine a beautiful Temple of our Lord God in heaven filled with black sooty smoke to demonstrated our Lord God's power and glory? Our Father has no darkness in Him. How could such a thing in heaven even happen, knowing the beauty in heaven which our Lord God loves to create. It would be a horrific site for the angels in heaven to see black sooty smoke billowing out from our Lord God's Temple. Also, notice it reads, our Lord God's Temple, and not our Lord God's Church. Our Lord God's Church is in heaven with our Lord Christ Jesus at the head. This is another reason we should doubt this chapter 15 is the complete Word of our Lord God. If you believe Satan will not use holy Scripture to his advantage then you should realize he regularly uses holy Scripture to convince others he is the Lord God. Satan used quotes from the holy Scripture to try and deceive Christ Jesus when he was being tempted by Satan for 40 days in the wilderness. Here is how that is described.

Luke 4:9-12

"Then the devil took him to Jerusalem, to the highest point of the Temple, and said, 'If you are the Son of God, jump off! For the Scriptures say, He will order his angels to protect and guard you. And they will hold you up with their hands so you won't even hurt your foot on a stone'(NLT).

Jesus responded, The Scriptures also says, 'You must not test the Lord your God'"(NLT).

Of course, our Lord Christ Jesus saw through Satan's attempts at deception; however, we often do not. As I said earlier, there is not much to chapter 15 that is of our Father in heaven, so let us move on to chapter 16.

The Seven Angels Pour Out the Seven Bowls Containing God's Wrath

In this chapter 16, we are confronted with seven bowls allegedly filled with our Lord God's wrath. However, as we know from our Lord Christ Jesus we have a very loving Lord God. So, let us keep that in mind as we read on.

Revelation 16:1

"Then I heard a mighty voice from the Temple say to the seven angels, 'Go your ways and pour out on the earth the seven bowls containing God's wrath'"(NLT).

The Seven Bowls Containing God's Wrath

Can you imagine what the angels in heaven must believe of our Father if He was to instruct His angels in heaven to pour out on the Earth all the plagues and earthquakes and other sufferings because He was outraged? Surely, our Lord

God would not want His angelic children to see all that was happening on Earth and all the suffering that was being caused due to His wrath upon the Earth even if it were true. Why would our Lord God allow the innocent angels in heaven to see such a horrific spectacle or even play a part in it, as a number of heavenly angels are alleged to have done. It is not likely our Father would ask His children in heaven, the holy angels, to do such horrible things to His other children on Earth.

Let Us Continue with the 7 Plagues Supposedly Poured Out by Our Fathers Angels

Revelation 16:2

"So the first angel left the Temple and poured out his bowl on the earth, and horrible, malignant sores broke out on everyone who had the mark of the beast and who worshiped his statue"(NLT).

Revelation 16:3

"Then the second angel poured out his bowl on the sea, and it became like the blood of a corpse. And everything in the sea died"(NLT).

Revelation 16:4-6

"Then the third angel poured out his bowl on the rivers and springs, and they became blood. And I heard the angel who had authority over all water saying, 'You are just, O Holy One, who is and who always was, because you have sent these judgments. Since they shed the blood of your holy people and your prophets, you have given them blood to drink. It is their just reward'"(NLT).

Revelation 16:7

"And, I heard a voice from the altar, saying, 'Yes, O Lord God, the Almighty, your judgments are true and just.'"(NLT).

Revelation 16:8-9

"Then the fourth angel poured out his bowl on the sun, causing it to scorch everyone with its fire. Everyone was burned by this blast of heat, and they cursed the name of God, who had control over all these plagues. They did not repent of their sins and turn to God and give him glory"(NLT).

Revelation 16:10-11

"Then the fifth angel poured out his bowl on the throne of the beast, and his kingdom was plunged into darkness. His subjects ground their teeth in anguish, and they cursed the God of heaven for their pains and sores. But they did not repent of their evil deeds and turn to God"(NLT).

Revelation 16:12-14

"Then the sixth angel poured out his bowl on the great Euphrates River, and it dried up so that the kings from the east could march their armies toward the west without hindrance. And I saw three evil spirits that looked like frogs leap from the mouths of the dragon, the beast, and the false prophet. They are demonic spirits who work miracles and go out to all the rulers of the world to gather them for battle against the Lord on that great judgment day of God the Almighty"(NLT).

We should not take this part of John's vision too seriously. The reason being, that Satan is the one behind all of the destruction mentioned in the verses above. Satan wants to put all the blame for the horrors above on our Lord God so all people on Earth will be terrified of Him. While all of what is written above is going on, what is Satan doing? Do you believe that Satan might be enjoying what he is seeing? I believe Satan would indeed. If our Lord God actually were to carry out such horrible acts, Satan would enjoy seeing all of the anguish, suffering, and death with relish.

After the seventh angel had poured out his bowl there was a loud sound of thunder, then a powerful earthquake shook the entire nation like none since humankind was first put upon the Earth. Nations crumbled due to the force of the earthquake and thousands of people died almost instantaneously. There were so many dead that nothing could be done for those who were trapped beneath the rubble. In due time, the whole nation fell silent as only a very few people survived the catastrophic earthquake. As time went slowly by, the nation slowly began to recover; however, it took many generations before the nation returned to a somewhat normal economy. So many people had died that only a few were strong and able enough to organize burial parties to begin to remove the remains from all of the buildings and homes destroyed in the earthquake. It would be many generations before the people felt safe in their homes once again. After more than seven generations had pass since the great earthquake the people erected a great wall to keep out invading armies. This was the beginning of a new Jerusalem that would stand for many centuries before it to was torn down by invading armies. They took down ever stone that was in the new Jerusalem and tossed them into the sea so that future generations would never be able to resurrect the original structure. After this there was relative peace for many generations and up unto the present time. The paragraph above was dictated to me by our Lord Christ Jesus.

As I explained before, 7 is an evil number in the context of the Book of Revelation and when you read the paragraphs above you see the evil they contain. Keep in mind our Lord God loves us more than we can possibly love ourselves or even our children, and there is no evil in Him. However, in the Book of Revelation we see a lot of evil being blamed on our Lord God. I shall continue to point this out as we continue our examination of the Book of Revelation.

Our Lord Christ Jesus Speaks of the End-of-Times

Our Lord Christ Jesus has always spoke of the end-of-times as coming soon. In this chapter 17, he speaks further and in depth to try and explain when the end-of-times will begin.

Revelation 17:1

"One of the seven angels who had poured out the seven bowls came over and spoke to me. 'Come with me,' he said, 'and I will show you the judgment that is going to come on the great prostitute, who rules over many waters'"(NLT).

Revelation 17:9-10

"This calls for a mind with understanding: The seven heads of the beast represent the seven hills where the woman rules. They also represent seven kings. Five kings have already fallen, the

sixth now reigns, and the seventh is yet to come, but his reign will be brief"(NLT).

The verses above once again have the number 7 and thus we should not pay them much attention. However, could the 7 hills tell us anything about the character of the beast? For example, could these first two verses be referring to the Holy See in Rome, Italy where Rome is built on 7 hills? Some speculate the Holy See is the city mention in the Book of Revelation 17:9-10. But when are these events to take place? Our Lord Christ Jesus said these events would take place "before this generation passes away," when Christ Jesus was speaking to his disciples in Jerusalem more than 1,990 years ago. Just below is what our Lord Christ Jesus stated that day concerning the end-of-days.

Matthew 24:1-2

"As Jesus was leaving the Temple grounds, his disciples pointed out to him the various Temple buildings. But he responded, 'Do you see all these building? I tell you the truth, they will be completely demolished. Not one stone will be left on top of another!'"(NLT).

This apparently happened when Jerusalem was overrun by enemies of Israel and they tore down the Temple in Jerusalem, one stone at a time. It has never been rebuilt to this day.

What is written above is in response to the question asked by his disciples. Let us read the entire account of what our Lord Christ Jesus said to his disciples on the day just mentioned. Matthew chapter 24 contains all of what he said. Let us begin there before we make any further judgments on the end-of-days.

Matthew 24:3

"Later, Jesus sat on the Mount of Olives. His disciples came to him privately and said, 'Tell us, when will all this happen? What sign will signal your return and the end of the world?'"(NLT).

Matthew 24:4-8

"Jesus told them, 'Don't let anyone mislead you, for many will come in my name, claiming, 'I am the Messiah.' They will deceive many. And you will hear of wars and threats of wars, but don't panic. Yes, these things must take place, but the end won't follow immediately. Nation will go to war against nation, and kingdom against kingdom. There will be famines and earthquakes in many parts of the world. But all this is only the birth pains, with more to come"(NLT).

Matthew 24:9-14

"Then you will be arrested, persecuted, and killed. You will be hated all over the world because you are my followers. And many will turn away from me and betray and hate each other. And many false prophets will appear and will deceive many people. Sin will be rampant everywhere, and the love of many will grow cold. But the one who endures to the end will be saved. And the Good News about the Kingdom will be preached throughout the whole world, so that all nations will hear it; and then the end will come"(NLT).

Our Lord Christ Jesus' Disciples Will Be Arrested, Persecuted, and Killed

In the last paragraph, our Lord Christ Jesus states to his disciples they would be arrested, persecuted, and killed. We know this did happen to his disciples and several were killed. Rome also persecuted thousands of Christians and burned some at the stake and some were thrown to the

Lions as the crowded amphitheater watched in horror. Could this be the period of persecution our Lord Christ Jesus was speaking of? Notice also that is says, "...and then the end will come." We find this at the bottom of the paragraph marked with the heading of Matthew 24:9-14. What exactly does this phrase mean? Might it mean the rapture would soon follow? Could it mean the end of the great persecution of Christians? Does it mean the end of the age? Or, does it mean the end-of-times, and exactly what does the end-of-times mean? The end of time and the end of Earth perhaps? This would mean total destruction of the Earth and everyone on it. It is not defined clearly in this holy Scripture, it only indicates something will happen once the Good News is spread throughout the world. Let us continue reading the holy Scripture that pertains to this subject.

Matthew 24:15-22

"The day is coming when you will see what Daniel the prophet spoke about--the sacrilegious object that causes desecration standing in the Holy Place. Then those in Judea must flee to the hills. A person out on the deck of a roof must not go down into the house to pack. A person out in the field must not return even to get a coat. How terrible it will be for pregnant women and for nursing mothers in those days. And pray that your flight will not be in winter or on the Sabbath. For there will be greater anguish than at any time since the world began. And it will never be so great again. In fact, unless that time of calamity is shortened, not a single person will survive. But it will be shortened for the sake of God's chosen ones"(NLT).

Sacrilegious Object Found in the Holy Place

Here we have another calamity which is about to unfold and it is triggered by a sacrilegious object being placed in the Holy Place. What might the Holy Place be other than The Holy of Holies. What object might it be? Whatever it may be, it suddenly sends people into a panic and our Lord Christ Jesus allegedly tells his disciples that everyone should drop what they are doing "...and flee to the hills." Christ Jesus also says that everyone in Judea must flee to the hills. He does not mention Israel or the surrounding nations.

There is no explanation as to why the people should flee to the hills. What safety will they find in the hills? Safety from perhaps an approaching flood? Perhaps an earthquake? Perhaps a volcanic eruption? There is no explanation why everyone should flee to the hills. Also, how are all of the people of that time to know some sacrilegious object has just been found in the Holy of Holies? Is the word going to spread instantaneously to all the people everywhere at once? If not, then the exodus from wherever the people are to the nearby hills will take place slowly as people hear, by word of mouth, that a sacrilegious object has been discovered in the Holy of Holies. Would it not seem simpler to just remove the sacrilegious object and discard it rather than cause a nationwide panic? However, I find this does not make sense to me unless more information was given as to the reason everyone must immediately flee to the hills and not take the time to pack. This indicates something very catastrophic is about to happen, but what?

The Holy of Holies No Longer Exists

Consider this, the Holy of Holies which housed the Arc of the Covenant no longer exists. Perhaps the desecration of the Holy of Holies took place when an invading army over a thousand years ago went into the Holy of Holies and took all the gold and silver and precious stones and left something crude behind in The Holy of Holies to demonstrate they would not be intimated by the God of Israel. So, this leads to the strong possibility the end-of-times happened sometime after our Lord Christ Jesus spoke to his disciples when he and his disciples were still alive and spreading the Good News. Let us continue reading.

Matthew 24:23-25

"Then if anyone tells you, 'Look, here is the Messiah,' or 'There he is,' don't believe it. For false messiahs and false prophets will rise up and perform great signs and wonders so as to deceive, if possible, even God's chosen ones. See, I have warned you about this ahead of time"(NLT).

See, I Have Warned You About This Ahead of Time

Does not the last sentence of the paragraph just above tell us Christ Jesus is warning his disciples about what is to come in their generation concerning the desecration of the Holy of Holies? It does sound like it. Christ Jesus is warning his disciples 'they must be on the watch' for what we have just read above concerning the Holy of Holies. Not centuries into the future, but while his disciples walked this Earth. Continuing on.

Matthew 24:26-28

"So if someone tells you, 'Look, the Messiah is out in the desert,' don't bother to go and look. Or, 'Look, he is hiding here,' don't believe it! For as the lightning flashes in the east and shines to the west, so it will be when the Son of Man comes. Just as the gathering of vultures shows there is a carcass nearby, so these signs indicate that the end is near"(NLT).

Matthew 24:29-31
"Immediately after the anguish of those days, the sun will be darkened, the moon will give no light, the stars will fall from the sky, and the power in the heavens will be shaken.

"And then at last, the sign that the Son of Man is coming will appear in the heavens, and there will be deep mourning among all the peoples of the earth. And they will see the Son of Man coming on the clouds of heaven with power and great glory. And he will send out his angels with the mighty blast of a trumpet, and they will gather his chosen ones from all over the world-from the farthest ends of the earth and heaven"(NLT).

Did the coming of the Lord already take place? Let us keep reading to find out.

Why would so many people on Earth be mourning on the day our Lord Christ Jesus returned to take all faithful Christians to heaven? Could it be due to the fact that many people will never see their loved ones again. Many people will simply disappear and be on Earth no longer, leaving many others behind. Others will know immediately with the coming of the Lord their lack of faith has condemned them. If you were left behind would you not be in mourning as well?

Matthew 24:32-35
"Now learn a lesson from the fig tree. When its branches bud and its leaves begin to sprout, you know that summer is near. In the same way, when you see all these things, you can know his return is very near, right at the door. I tell you the truth, this generation will not pass from the scene until all these things take place. Heaven and earth will disappear but my words will never disappear"(NLT).

In the paragraph above our Lord Christ Jesus says to all of the disciples present this: "I tell you the truth, this generation will not pass from the scene until all these things take place." This sentence says very clearly the events our Lord Christ Jesus has been speaking of to his disciples will occur 'before their generation passes from the scene.' So, if we are to take what our Lord Christ Jesus stated to his disciples concerning the end of the world truthfully, then the end-of-time has already taken place. This means the rapture has occurred and we, those of us living at this present time, are the ones who have been left behind and many generations before us.

For those of you who may not know, the Temple in Jerusalem was destroyed by the Romans in 70 AD. That is when the dispersion of the Jews took place and they went to various places around the world. Then in 1948 the Jews forced the Palestinian people off their lands and established the present-day nation of Israel. The Palestinian people remain in walled camps and cities to this very day as more and more of their land is stolen from them. The United States is one of the very few nations who could help the Palestinian people to be free once again. It would be to the United States benefit if they would stand with the Palestinian people and insist that Israel free the Palestinian people and cease occupying their lands. This is something our Lord Christ Jesus would like to see happen.

Now, back to where we were looking at the explanation of the end-of-times.

Matthew 24:34-35

"I tell you the truth, this generation will not pass from the scene until all these things take place. Heaven and earth will disappear, but my words will never disappear"(NLT).

Matthew 24:37-39

"When the Son of Man returns, it will be like it was in Noah's day. In those days before the flood, the people were enjoying banquets and parties and weddings right up to the time Noah entered his boat. People didn't realize what was going to happen until the flood came and swept them all away. That is the way it will be when the Son of Man comes"(NLT).

That is the Way It Will Be When the Son of Man Comes

If our Lord Christ Jesus has already come and raptured those who were his followers and we are the ones who were left behind, then what must we do to gain salvation and be taken home to heaven? First, we must remain faithful and loyal to our Lord God and our Lord Christ Jesus and face whatever tribulations Satan has in store for us and not turn away from our Lord God during that time. Second, listen to The Holy Spirit from within. Third, know that our Lord God is not the one causing all the tribulations we are having to endure. Fourth, we should pray for our protection from the coming tribulations, in groups if possible.

According to our Lord Christ Jesus the end times has already taken place. Christ Jesus said "I tell you the truth, this generation will not pass from the scene until all these things take place." So, we should begin to believe in our Lord Christ Jesus and take up his cross and follow him if we have not already done so. It would seem a wise thing to do.

CHAPTER 18

The Great City is Fallen!

In this chapter 18, what might this chapter represent other than the total collapse of the world financial system. All of the foreign merchants are in great fear and awe of the total destruction of Babylon. The great city has fallen, now what will happen to them? The great city supplied the world with every imaginable product. From textiles to sex slaves. With this chapter begins the story of the fall of Babylon.

Revelation 18:1

"After all this I saw another angel come down from heaven with great authority, and the earth grew bright with splendor. He gave a mighty shout: 'Babylon is fallen—that great city is fallen!' She has become a home for demons. She is a hideout for every foul spirit, a hideout for every foul vulture and every fowl and dreadful animal. For all the nations have fallen because of the wine of her passionate immorality: The Kings of the world have committed adultery with her. Because of her desires of extravagant luxury, the merchants of the world have grown rich"(NLT).

Revelation 18:4-8

"Then I heard another voice calling from heaven, 'Come away from her, my people. Do not take part in her sins, or you will be punished with her. For her sins are piled as high as heaven, and God remembers her evil deeds. Do to her as she has done to others. Double her penalty for all her evil deeds. She brewed a cup of terror for others, so brew twice as much for her. She glorified herself and lived in luxury, so match it now with torment and sorrow. She boasted in her heart, 'I am queen on my throne. I am no helpless widow, and I have no reason to mourn.' Therefore, these plagues will overtake her in a single day-death and morning and famine. She will be completely consumed by fire, for the Lord God who judges her is mighty'"(NLT).

Revelation 18:9-10

"And the kings of the world who committed adultery with her and enjoyed her great luxury will morn for her as they see the smoke rising from her charred remains. They will stand at a distance, terrified by her great torment. They will cry out, 'How terrible, how terrible for you, O Babylon, you great city! In a single moment God's judgment came on you'"(NLT).

Could this verse just above be suggesting that perhaps a nuclear bomb may have destroyed the city of Babylon? What else could destroy so thoroughly a huge city which Babylon must have been? However, is Babylon in Iraq or is it some other city? Present day Babylon is not nearly as rich as the city of Babylon portrayed in the holy Scripture. It would have had to be a major port city to transport so many goods all over the world. How much sorrow and fear would there be if present day Babylon, Iraq were to suddenly exist no more? It would be a surprise to everyone and many people would mourn the loss of Babylon, Iraq. However, it would not send shockwaves around the world to all the world's merchants like the destruction of the city of Babylon mentioned in the Book of Revelation must have. Has the destruction of Babylon come to pass or is it yet to be? There are four major port cities that would be missed terribly by the rest of the world. They are New York City, London, England, Singapore, China, and Durban, South Africa. The one that would be missed by most of the world would be, in my opinion, the port city of New York City. We know that New York City is still going strong and I do not know of any major port city that has been destroyed by fire, so it is safe to say that the Babylon in the holy Scriptures has not yet been destroyed by fire.

Revelation 18:11-13

"The merchants of the world will weep and mourn for her, for there is no one left to buy their goods. She bought great quantities of gold, silver, jewels, and pearls; fine linen, purple silk, and scarlet cloth; things made of fragrant thyine wood, ivory goods, and objects made of expensive wood; and bronze, iron, and marble. She also bought cinnamon, spice, incense, myrrh, frankincense, wine, olive oil, fine flour, wheat, cattle, sheep, horses, wagons, and bodies-that is, human slaves"(NLT).

Revelation 18:14-17

"The fancy things you loved so much are gone," they cry. "All your luxuries and splendor are gone forever, never to be yours again.

"The merchants who became wealthy by selling her these things will stand at a distance, terrified by her great torment. They will weep and cry out, 'How terrible, how terrible for that great city! She was clothed in finest purple and scarlet linens, decked out with gold and precious stones and pearls! In a single moment all the wealth of the city is gone!'"(NLT).

Revelations 18:18-20

"And all the captains of the merchant ships and their passengers and sailors and crews will stand at a distance. They will cry out as they watch the smoke ascend, and they will say, 'Where is there another city as great as this?' And they will weep and throw dust on their heads to show their grief. And they will cry out, 'How terrible, how terrible for that great city! The shipowners became wealthy by transporting her great wealth on the seas. In a single moment it is all gone.' Rejoice over her fate, O heaven and people of God and apostles and prophets! For at last God has judged her for your sakes"(NLT).

In the verses just above it reads, "In a single moment it is all gone," suggesting to me once again that Babylon was very likely struck with a nuclear bomb which would devastate any city in a single moment of time and leave it burning in its own ashes. In the paragraph after, an angel of our Lord God picked up a boulder the size of a millstone and hurled it into the sea. Then the angel stated that never again would the great city of Babylon ever exist. It will be thrown down with violence never to be seen again. Never will there be the sound of harps, happy voices, musical instruments, happy occasions, singers, flutes, or trumpets. Neither will there be merchants, craftsmen, or trades of any kind. Babylon will never exist again and never will there be another city to replace it in jewels, gold and silver, precious stones, silk, aromatic wood, flour, sugar, salt, animals such as horses, donkeys, goats, sheep, and cattle, and all the other items that a rich society might have. No longer will people be bought and sold like cattle. No longer will there be ships filling its harbor, nor men to man those ships. Never will there be the smell of the granaries or the mills to turn grains into flour to prepare bountiful breads. Never again will merchants barter for goods and services. Never again will there be dancing in the streets. Sorcery deceived many people and their wicked ways caused many to stray from our Lord God. Never again will there be lights in the streets. Babylon's streets ran red with the blood of our Lord God's children and the holy prophets and the blood of people slaughtered all over the world. Thus, ends the great city of Babylon.

What are we to make of this chapter which is void of the number 7? Perhaps this chapter was not influenced by Satan and what we read here may be true. Also, perhaps that Babylon is not in Iraq, but somewhere else in the world and it is a major city with a major seaport and it is full of sin and sells every form of luxury. Not only that, it also deals in human slavery. Perhaps this is why this city met the fate it does. I believe we can take this chapter 18 to be something to look for in our not so distant future. Thus, ends chapter 18. Now, let us move on to chapter 19.

The False Prophet and the Beast Are Thrown into Hell

In this chapter 19 we finally see justice being done when the beast and the false prophet are both thrown into hell for all eternity.

Revelation 19:20

"And the beast was captured and with him the false prophet who did mighty miracles on behalf of the beast—miracles that deceived all who accepted the mark of the beast and who worshiped his statue. Both the beast and his false prophet were thrown alive into the fiery lake of burning sulfur"(NLT).

Chapter 19 verse 20 speaks of the beast being captured and thrown into hell along with the false prophet. So, this is not Satan himself. Instead, it is the beast that Satan created. Who or what might this beast be? This remains to be seen. Still, overall, this chapter 19 speaks of the end of Satan's rule on Earth. Some believe that Satan was defeated at the cross. However, there is no holy Scripture that verifies that belief. Instead, we see that Satan is still ruling this world with an iron fist and destroying nation after nation. Think of all the nations who have been destroyed in the last few hundred years. The Indian nations of North America, the nation of Iraq, the nation of Libya, the nation of Syria, the nation of Yemen, the nation of Ukraine, and others that once existed but no longer do. Satan is still at work in this world and we see it now in what is happening to the greatest nation of all time. We speak of the United States. The United States is being divided into multiple political ideologies. If the United States does not turn to our Lord God soon, then we may be one more nation that was brought down by Satan. He has long targeted the United States simply due to the fact the United States has long been a largely Christian nation. However, today our leaders are more concerned with political influence and receiving campaign contributions which can cost in the millions of dollars. No longer do our nation's leaders care much what the voting people need. They know they can do pretty much whatever they want and still not be held accountable. However, if the American people would humble themselves before our Lord God and ask for forgiveness for what they have done to their nation, our Lord God would forgive them and help them to begin moving in a righteous direction once again. For example, it has been almost 80 years since Congress last declared war which is their constitutional duty. Today, our President can start an undeclared war anytime he sees fit and Congress will not hold him accountable. Ukraine is a perfect example of this where we have recently been told that U.S. Troops are in Ukraine serving in combat positions. Elsewhere, President Biden is instigating the start of another military conflict in Taiwan since he has unilaterally decided that Taiwan is an independent nation and is not part of Communist China.

Congress allows our President's to start undeclared wars due to the fact that to oppose the president on matters of foreign war would mean that members of Congress may not receive the huge sums of campaigns funds they would get from the military industrial complex which makes huge profits during military conflicts. Not to mention all the armaments they sell to nations friendly to the United States and our allies.

We include the above, since we are dangerously close to losing our freedoms. If we were to enter into a major military conflict with Russia or Communist China or both, our government would most likely use the military conflict to declare martial law and take more of our freedoms and liberties away and no one would be allowed to speak against such wars.

Have you noticed how our government uses war as an excuse to further restrict our rights. This may be why our government is now trying to provoke Russia into further escalating the current crisis in Ukraine. The Patriot Act was a major blow to our freedoms and Congress continues to renew it each time it comes up for a vote. Then the Covid pandemic came along and we lost even more of our civil rights and we were even locked down in our homes. Many people lost their businesses and jobs and never got them back. And, they lied about the source of SARS-CoV-2 which causes Covid. If you want to save our nation, then get down on your knees and ask our Father in heaven to forgive us for our not standing up for our rights for so long. This is all I have to say on this subject except to say that Satan is not resting.

CHAPTER 20

Satan is Bound in Chains for a Thousand Years

In this chapter 20, Satan is bound by an angel of our Lord God for a thousand years. After the thousand years has passed Satan will be freed for a short while.

Revelation 20:1-2

"Then I saw an angel coming down from heaven with a key to the bottomless pit and a heavy chain in his hand. He seized the dragon—that old serpent, who is the devil, Satan—and bound him in chains for a thousand years"(NLT).

Satan Is Bound in Chains for a Thousand Years

In this chapter we discover that Satan is placed in chains and shackled and thrown into the bottomless pit for a thousand years, before he is released again for a short time. How would you like to be bound in chains and shackled in place for a thousand years? And, in the dark. Not a pleasant thing to contemplate is it? It would be especially difficult for Satan who is always commanding his demons to attack and hurt our Father's children.

Revelation 20:4

"Then I saw thrones, and the people sitting on them had been given the authority to judge. And I saw the souls of those who had been beheaded for their testimony about Jesus and for proclaiming the word of God. They had not worshiped the beast or his statue, nor accepted the mark on their foreheads or their hands. They all came to life again, and they reigned with Christ for a thousand years"(NLT).

What does the above Scripture mean? It means that all those who had died by having their heads removed have been waiting in purgatory until the day they would return once again and be reborn into new bodies on the Earth. These are the ones who never denied our Lord Christ and were beheaded for their refusal to deny our Lord Christ Jesus. My thought is this, why did they not go to heaven if they were such faithful and devout Christians? If anyone could make it to heaven, surely, they should have. That is all I have to say on that matter.

They Will Reign on Earth with our Lord Christ Jesus For a Thousand Years

Then they will reign with our Lord Christ Jesus on Earth for a thousand years. After the thousand years has ended Satan will be released and he will confront the nations of Gog and Magog on Earth and deceive these two nations into following him. Satan is known as the great deceiver and he will once again deceive much of the human race on Earth to yet, once again, turn their backs on Christ Jesus and our Father in heaven and attack Jerusalem in a futile attempt to overthrow our Lord God once again. The armies

Satan raises will be utterly destroyed by fire from heaven and then, Satan will be thrown into the lake of fire with the beast and the false prophet to suffer greatly for some very long period of time only our Lord God knows. However, it will not be for all time or forever. Our Lord God is merciful and He will once again give Satan the opportunity to accept our Lord Christ Jesus as his Lord and Savior.

Satan Will Burn in Hell for Each of Those He Sent to Hell

Imagine what it would be like to burn in a fiery lake of fire for all time without ever being given a chance to repent. It would not be right to have to burn for all time and our Lord God is just. Satan will have to suffer the same suffering he caused others and when he has suffered for a very long period of time, then our Lord God will give Satan the opportunity to join everyone else in heaven, if Satan will accept our Lord Christ Jesus as his Lord and Savior. Perhaps he will or perhaps he will not. However, he will have experienced all the suffering he caused all those he threw into the fiery lake of fire and all the pain and suffering he caused others on Earth during their lifetimes. By then Satan may have realized all his efforts to be lord and master of the human race were in vain.

Again, imagine what it will be like for Satan to experience the suffering he caused all of humanity one lifetime at a time. What I mean by this is Satan will live the lives of all those people who have lived on Earth and who suffered terribly in their lives and even those who did not suffer all that much but still fell victim to Satan's attacks in their lives. Satan will be forced to live billions of lifetimes and experience the suffering as it was experienced for each of the billions of people he ruled over. Including burning in hell for a thousand years or more for each one Satan cast into hell. And, he will have to experience personally the lives of those same people and experience their lives and suffer the way they did. Suffering caused by Satan himself. Satan will feel the love their parents or spouses or friends and family had for them. He will experience their fears and worries and concerns and all that someone may experience in a lifetime. In this way, he will begin to see for himself how he affected the lives of others and what it felt like to be loved. Something that Satan has not experienced for tens of millions of years. Eventually, it is our Lord God's hope that Satan will then have developed the soul to feel remorse and sorrow for what he has done to all of humanity. Much like it happens to each of us; however, that is a story for another time.

Satan Returns to Earth for a Short While

It is clear that after Satan is released from his one-thousand-year sentence in the bottomless pit, he will return to Earth for only a short while. He will deceive Gog and Magog, two nations on Earth, into following him. This is not to say these are the only two nations on Earth. Only that these two nations Satan will be able to deceive into following him and attacking new Jerusalem. Satan and his army will be utterly destroyed as our Lord God calls for fire from heaven to rain down on Satan and his army and in the end Satan's army will be completely wiped out. Then Satan will be caste into the lake of fire to suffer for many eternities. Thus, ends Satan's rule on Earth for all time.

A New Heaven and a New Earth

Chapter 21 of the Book of Revelation is about a new relationship with our Lord God and our Lord Christ Jesus. Let us begin.

Revelation 21:1-2

"Then I saw a new heaven and a new earth, for the old heaven and the old earth had disappeared. And the sea was also gone. And I saw the holy city, the new Jerusalem, coming down from God out of heaven like a new bride beautifully dressed for her husband"(NLT).

Revelation 21:3-4

"I heard a loud shout from the throne, saying, 'Look, God's home is now among his people! He will live with them, and they will be his people. God himself will be with them. He will wipe every tear from their eyes, and there will be no more death or sorrow or crying or pain. All these things are gone forever.'"

Revelation 21:5-7

"And the one sitting on the throne said, 'Look, I am making everything new!' And then he said to me, 'Write this down, for what I tell you is trustworthy and true.' And he also said, 'It is finished! I am the Alpha and the Omega-the Beginning and the End. To all who are thirsty I will give freely from the springs of the water of life. All who are victorious will inherit all these blessings, and I will be their God, and they will be my children"(NLT).

Revelation 21:8

"But cowards, unbelievers, the corrupt, murderers, the immoral, those who practice witchcraft, idol worshipers, and all liars-their fate is in the fiery lake of burning sulfur. This is the second death'"(NLT).

Revelation 21:9

"Then one of the seven angels who held the seven bowls containing the seven last plagues came and said to me. 'Come with me! I will show you the bride, the wife of the Lamb'"(NLT).

Revelation 21:10-14

"So he took me in the Spirit to a great, high mountain, and he showed me the holy city, Jerusalem, descending out of heaven from God. It shone with the glory of God and sparkled like a precious stone-like jasper as clear as crystal. The city wall was high and broad, with twelve gates guarded by twelve angels. And the names of the twelve tribes of Israel were written on the gates. There were three gates on each side—east, north, south and west. The wall of the city had twelve foundation stones, and on them were written the names of the twelve apostles of the Lamb"(NLT).

Revelation 21:15-17

"The angel who talked to me held in his hand a gold measuring stick to measure the city, its gates, and its wall. When he measured it, he found it was a square, as wide as it was long. In fact, its length and width and height were each 1,400 miles. Then he measured the walls and found them to be 216 feet thick (according to the human standard used by the angel)"(NLT).

Revelation 21:18-20

"The wall was made of jasper, and the city was pure gold, as clear as glass. The wall of the city was built on foundation stones inlaid with twelve precious stones: the first was jasper, the second sapphire, the third agate, the fourth emerald, the fifth onyx, the sixth carnelian, the seventh chrysolite, the eight beryl, the ninth topaz, the tenth chrysoprase, the eleventh jacinth, the twelfth amethyst"(NLT).

I recently read in a chemistry text book that gold can be hammered into sheets so thin that you can see through it. The chemistry text book I have, shows an illustration of a burning candle behind a very thin sheet of gold foil. I could actually see the candle and the burning flame behind the gold foil.

Revelation 21:21

"The twelve gates were made of pearls--each gate from a single pearl! And the main street was pure gold, as clear as glass"(NLT).

Imagine a pearl big enough to allow you to carve out a huge door from one single pearl. That is one huge pearl shell. I wonder what the pearl must look like with a shell that large? Beautiful and lustrous, I am sure. Anyway, what can we make of these few verses. It seems clear that twelve is a holy number since it is used in very specific cases. For instance, the 12-year-old girl brought back to life. Or, the

12-year-old boy also brought back to life. The 12 ounces of perfume poured over the head of our Lord Christ Jesus. The 12 years the woman suffered from constant bleeding, the 12 apostles, the 12 tribes, the 12 foundation stones, and the 12 gates to new Jerusalem.

There Will Be No Sun or Moon on New Earth

On the new Earth there will be no stars or moon to give light. The brilliance of the day will be due to the presence of our Lord God who will shine even brighter than the sun did on old Earth. Another source of light will radiate from our Lord Christ Jesus who will be with us on the new Earth as is our Father in heaven. The holy Scriptures tell us there will be no sun as we have on Earth and there will be no night on new Earth, only the light from our Father and our Lord Christ Jesus will light the city of new Jerusalem and new Earth as well.

In the new Jerusalem there will be many who will come trying to gain entry only to be turned away by angels who guards the twelve gates leading into new Jerusalem. Our Lord God will not tolerate those who are sorcerers, those who delve in witchcraft or other practices of the black arts. It is hard to imagine that people like those just mentioned will still exist in new Jerusalem and new Earth, but apparently, they will. Why would our Lord God allow such people onto the new Earth? Perhaps because our Lord God knows that one day these people who are not allowed to enter new Jerusalem will one day repent, accept our Lord Christ Jesus as their Lord and Savior and become one of his disciples.

Idolaters will also not be allowed to enter new Jerusalem. Nor anyone who practices dishonest behavior. This means that new Jerusalem will be a perfectly run place for our Lord God's children to visit and live. As we found out earlier, there are trillions of rooms in new Jerusalem where we can live and probably work as well. And, those who live in the upper stories of new Jerusalem will have a fantastic view since they will peer out windows that are miles above the surface of new Earth. Not only that, many will live high enough up in new Jerusalem to be in outer space. They will see the most beautiful heavens than you can imagine just outside their front window and not worry that the window might get hit by an asteroid or comet. It will be perfectly safe since our Lord God himself made new Jerusalem and we know He can make no mistakes. He can also deflect them away from new Jerusalem since He will be there protecting us.

One day new Jerusalem will be removed from new Earth after everyone has accepted our Lord Christ Jesus as their Lord and Savior. Then new Jerusalem will be taken to heaven and remain there for all eternity to show the history of Earth and its people.

Why Is There No Mention of Heaven?

Still, in all of the Book of Revelation there is no mention of a heaven where we all go except when the rapture took place. So, let us assume the people still living on new Earth have still not accepted our Lord Christ Jesus as their Lord and Savior. What else could explain the reason people on new Earth have not yet gone to heaven? What we see here is the angels our Lord God created and which later followed Satan and were thrown down to Earth with Satan are still being given chance after chance after chance to accept our Lord God as their Lord and Savior. Until they do so they will continue to live on new Earth until the day they finally accept our Lord Christ Jesus as their Lord and Savior. Perhaps these people are the hardest of hardest as we might say and their hearts are still very hard due to their close association with Satan. Even though they live in the presence of our Father and His Son, still there are people on new Earth that are resistant to their presence and are still rejecting our Lord Christ Jesus and our Father in heaven. They are still not yet ready to give up the delights of the flesh or the cravings of the flesh, or their desire to have power and control over others. This is why not everyone will be able to enter the new Jerusalem and why there are angels guarding each gate of new Jerusalem. And, the Book of Life is still present as well.

Our Lord God Has Removed Satan's Evil Influence

By removing the presence of Satan in the lives of his children on new Earth, our Lord God has greatly enhanced their chances of being redeemed from Satan's influence in their lives. Eventually, every single one of our Father's children will accept our Lord Christ Jesus as their Lord and Savior and will finally return home. When that day comes it will be a great day in heaven. There is one item that I would to add. I felt it was best to include the holy Scripture below at this point in my book. I believe you will find it very interesting.

The Mind-Boggling Dimensions of New Jerusalem

As I was reading along in chapter 21 of the Book of Revelation I noticed the dimensions of new Jerusalem. I will be paraphrasing Revelation 21:15-17. My paraphrase version begins as follows: The angel took John to a high mountain to see the holy City. As the apostle John watched the angel who held a gold measuring stick, the angel began to measure the dimensions of new Jerusalem. Then the angel asked John to write down its dimensions; the length, width, and height. When the angel measured it, he found it was a square, as wide as it was long. The angel found the walls to be the same length, width, and height; 1400 miles. Actually, it was measured in stadia and not miles. I converted stadia into miles to make it easier for my readers to understand its true dimensions. Actually, 1400 miles is equal to 12000 stadia. This can be found in the footnotes of Tyndale's New Living Translation Life Application Study Bible of the holy Scriptures which is where I find all of my holy Scripture references as well.

If we multiply 12000 stadia by 12000 stadia it will give the square stadia inside the walls of new Jerusalem. It shows to be 144,000,000 square stadia. When the angel measured the thickness of the wall, he found it to be 216 feet thick. If we add the figures in 216, we get 2 + 1 + 6 = 9. According to my copy of the holy Scriptures, 216 feet is equivalent to 144 cubits. Again, 1 + 4 + 4 = 9. So, as you can see, 3 and 9 play an important role in the construction of new Jerusalem and perhaps in the very design of the universe as well. Nicola Tesla had a theory called the 369 theory of the universe. I will provide a link below that will explain Tesla's theory in more detail. According to Nicola Tesla's theory, the universe relies on the figures 3, 6, and 9 to construct every object in the universe. Tesla proved this mathematically.

The YouTube hyperlink at the end of this paragraph is from "Engineering Made Easy" which explains Nicola Tesla's 369 theory. However, I have not been able to find a name associated with this website. Whoever the author is he did an amazing job of describing the importance of the number 9, more so than 3 or 6. Below are two hyperlinks that will help you better understand why the holy Scriptures contain many references to multiples of 3, which I have shown in a previous chapter.

https://www.youtube.com/watch?v=YnMFQFDhy-4

The above video hyperlink was based on the writings of Dejan Davcevski. You can find the written article he wrote concerning Tesla's 369 theory on the link just below.

https://www.lifecoachcode.com/2016/10/11/the-secret-behind-3-6-9-revealed/

In some respects, you may prefer reading Mr. Davcevski's written article over the video if you prefer written explanations. They can often be clearer; however, Mr. Davcevski's writing does not cover as much concerning the number 9 as does the video.

Let us get back to new Jerusalem. Can you imagine seeing a structure so large that it stretches far beyond our vision in all directions? New Jerusalem is 1400 miles wide, 1400 miles in length, and 1400 miles in height. If we stood on top of this 1400-mile structure we would be standing in outer space. Our atmosphere is only a few hundred miles thick, so at the very top of new Jerusalem we are higher above the surface of Earth than the International Space Station height in orbit. However, we do not know how thick the atmosphere of new Earth might be. So, let us keep that in mind.

If we were at the very top of new Jerusalem we would be looking down upon the International Space Station over a thousand miles below us. Is that not truly an amazing height? Only our Lord God could build a structure this gargantuan in size! Can you imagine what a sight it will be for those on new Earth who will be the first to see this incredible structure? Eye-popping in size! Then our Lord God will gently sit new Jerusalem down on some lovely spot on new Earth. Our Lord God is mighty strong to do such a thing. And, all of its inhabitants will be able to come and go as they please. Later, I will describe in even more detail how there are 12 gates, with 3 gates on each side of the city. But first, let us try to determine how many rooms this amazing city might have.

Four-Thousand-Thirty-Nine Trillion Rooms in New Jerusalem

New Jerusalem is 1400 miles by 1400 miles by 1400 miles which gives us 2,744,000,000 cubic miles. Now, if we take 5280 ft. x 5280 ft. x 5280 ft. this will give us 147,197,952,000 cubic ft. in one cubic mile. Let us suppose that one room is 100 ft. x 100 ft. x 10 ft, which equals 100,000 cubic ft. If we now divide 147,197,952,000 cubic ft., - which is our one cubic mile calculated above - by 100,000 cubic ft., we get 1,471,979.52 rooms of 100,000 cubic feet. There are 2,744,000,000 cubic miles in new Jerusalem which was calculated near the beginning of this chapter. If we now multiply the number of rooms in one cubic mile, which is 1,471,980 roughly by the number of cubic miles in new Jerusalem, it will give us the total number of rooms that are 100 ft. by 100 ft. by 10 ft. Here is how that calculation looks: 2,744,000,000 cubic miles multiplied by 1,471,980 rooms in one cubic mile gives us; 4039 trillion rooms in new Jerusalem. This is a staggering number of rooms! Our Father in heaven has made room for each of us and then some. If we write out that number it looks like this; 4,039,113,120,000,000 rooms approximately in new Jerusalem. Once again, this is roughly 4039 trillion rooms. A trillion is 1 x 10 to the power of 12. Keep in mind that each of these 4039 trillion rooms are 100 ft. by 100 ft. by 10 ft. This is one very large room. Each 100 ft. by 100 ft. by 10 ft. room is approximately 1/5 the size of a football field. This is about the size of a mansion. Would you not like to move into new Jerusalem and have our Lord God specially design your room to fit who you are? I believe it would be a truly amazing experience. Also, would it not be interesting to visit our neighbors' rooms and their friends' rooms to see how each room is especially decorated by our Lord God, just for them?

Now, getting back to our calculations, if we multiply 12000 stadia by 12000 stadia by 12000 stadia we get 1,728,000,000,000 square stadia. When we add these numbers together we get: $1 + 7 + 2 + 8 + 0 + 0 + 0 + 0 + 0 + 0 + 0 + 0 + 0 = 18 = 1 + 8 = 9$. The same situation is also true for the number of rooms in new Jerusalem which we calculated to be 4,039,113,120,000,000. When we add each of these individual numbers together we arrive at: $4 + 0 + 3 + 9 + 1 + 1 + 3 + 1 + 2 + 0 + 0 + 0 + 0 + 0 + 0 + 0 = 24 = 2 + 4 = 6$, which is a holy number being a multiple of 3. Is this not interesting.

The Holy Trinity: The Father, the Son, and The Holy Spirit

If you recall, when we first multiplied 12,000 stadia by 12,000 stadia we came up with 144,000,000. When we add the figures in 144,000,000 together we end up with: $1 + 4 + 4 + 0 + 0 + 0 + 0 + 0 + 0 = 9$. And, if you add up the numbers in 12000 stadia, $1 + 2 + 0 + 0 + 0 = 3$. It does seem our Lord God likes to build using multiples of 3, which is not so strange when you remember the Holy Trinity of our Lord God. The Father, the Son, and The Holy Spirit.

What are we to discern from chapter 21? Suddenly we are seeing new Jerusalem in all its glory. What a magnificent structure it will be. Any earthly engineer would not be able to conceive of such a monumental task as designing or creating such a massive structure with all of the fixtures and precious stones and windows, doors, water fountains and water basins. And, what of the plumbing for such a mind-boggling structure? It would require millions of miles of plumbing. Can you imagine a contractor getting the contract to install this much piping and getting everything to work as it should? Including all of the toilets. How would you ever get them all to work properly? This would be a hydrologists nightmare! Thankfully, this will not happen since our Lord God will do all the necessary plumbing and, more than likely, it will not be anything like we are accustomed to. It will be far more than we could ever imagine. In fact, it probably will not have toilets at all, since that would make our Lord God's home very unsanitary for Him. What would there be instead? I guess we will have to wait and see.

Let me give you this bit of information concerning our Lord Christ Jesus who was nailed to the Cross. Our Lord Christ Jesus' left hand was at the 3 o'clock position, his feet were at the 6 o'clock position, his right hand was at the 9 o'clock position, and his head at the 12 o'clock position. This is why the numbers of 3, 6, 9, and 12 are considered holy numbers and all are multiples of 3.

CHAPTER 22

The New Earth

The new Earth has finally arrived in this chapter 22. You might be surprised just what the new Jerusalem really is. It is often overlooked; however, in this chapter you will know more than you thought probable.

Revelation 22:2
"On each side of the river grew a tree of life, bearing twelve crops of fruit, with a fresh crop each month. The leaves were used for medicine to heal the nations"(NLT).

According to what is written in chapter 22:2, our Lord God and our Lord Christ Jesus will have thrones on the new Earth. All the servants living with them will worship them and they will live in the presence of our Lord God and our Lord Christ Jesus. The Lord God will provide all the light we need and His light will shine continuously. There will be no need for lamps since the light of our Lord God will provide light even behind walls. There will be no darkness anywhere. Much like it is in heaven. There will be no need for the scorching rays of the sun and there will be no moon to light the night. Will there be stars to view? This, the holy Scriptures do not tell us. Our Lord God and our Lord Christ Jesus shall reign forever and ever. An angel of our Father was sent to tell us that everything we have heard and seen is trustworthy and true. The angel was sent to tell us what will happen next.

Is everything we have read in Revelation trustworthy and true? I will leave it up to the reader to decide. The holy Scripture in the Book of Revelation chapter 22 continues with a message that Jesus is coming soon. And it says that anyone who obeys the words written in the Book of Revelation are blessed. The angel of our Father then tells John to not seal up the words in the Book of Revelation for the time is near. Then the angel delivers more words form our Lord Christ Jesus that states he will be coming soon bringing a reward to repay his people and their deeds. Near the end of chapter 22 a warning is given. It reads as follows.

Revelation 22:18-19

"And I solemnly declare to everyone who hears the words of prophecy written in this book: If anyone adds anything to what is written here. God will add to that person the plagues described in the book. And if anyone removes any of the words from this book of prophecy, God will remove that person's share in the tree of life and in the holy city that are described in this book"(NLT).

This is a very frightening warning and I am taking a chance that what is written here is a warning from Satan and not a warning from our Father in heaven. However, I believe it is important to point out that Satan had a hand in distorting the truth that our Lord Christ Jesus intended for us to have and has instead twisted it to frighten and confuse us about the love our Father in heaven really has for us. Satan hopes that after we read Revelation we will doubt what love is and doubt if our Creator and Father really loves us at all. How do you feel after reading Revelation? Do you feel frightened and confused or do you feel comforted by what you have read? Many of the quotes we have read in Revelation actually come from the Old Testament. In fact, almost all of Revelation seems to have been written for those of the Jewish faith. Not once is the word, Christian, seen in the text. It does mention our Lord God's holy people which usually refers to the twelve tribes of Israel. The Book of Revelation does leave one to wonder who the Book of Revelation was written for; Christian or Jew.

Before we continue, I would like to take you on a side journey and explain what the new Earth will be like. The information that follows was given to me by our Lord Christ Jesus and I believe it to be true.

To begin, Christ Jesus said to me that the new Earth will not be a place for those who betrayed their Lord God. Instead, it will be a place where many people live and work and farm and ranch. Others will be business managers, corporate executives, politicians, government agents, lawyers, doctors, dentists, etc. No one will be required to pay taxes since the monetary system will be set up to benefit the people and not take advantage of them. The President of whatever nation on new Earth we may be living in will be fair minded and work for the people and not for special interests. The people of new Earth will live lives similar to what we live on Earth today; but, their lives will be peaceful and productive and free above all else. One day, our Lord God will ask all of us on new Earth to help one another to solve our social issues. Committees will be formed which will hear both sides of the issue and suggest remedies for the minor problems inhabitants of new Earth will have. The committees will make very wise decisions which will help a majority of people. No one will be left out of the decision-making process and everyone will be greatly helpful during the process. No one will ever prosper more than the other people involved with the decision-making process. All will benefit and more people will want to get involved so they can help others benefit from the decisions made. New Earth will be a unique world and nearly everyone will be happy with life on new Earth.

There Will Be Sorcerers, the Sexually Immoral, the Murderers, the Idol Worshipers, and All Who Love to Live a Lie

However, there will be a few who will not be willing to cooperate with all the other new earthers. They will be the sorcerers, the sexually immoral, the murderers, the idol worshipers, and all who love to live a lie. The above sentence is taken from the Book of Revelation 22:15. Also, there will be those who try to overthrow the existing authority. They will not succeed since there will be far too few of them. They would like to overthrow the existing authority since they are disciples of Satan who is, at that time, burning alive in hell along with his demons. Satan's incarceration in hell will make it very difficult for anyone to overthrow the existing authority. In fact, it is near impossible since everyone on new Earth will know full well that Satan is the one who instigated governmental overthrows and will not be able to help the evil doers on new Earth. Most will be viewed as outsiders and will not be able to find the help they need to successfully overthrow said authority. They will eventually decide to isolate themselves in one area of new Earth. These people will call themselves followers of Satan; however, in time they give in to the majority of people and will begin to live a more fruitful life. One day, a man will come along who will help the remnant followers of Satan find a better way to live their lives. After all, they are living in a world where few problems exist, yet their minds are still craving the things of this world and not the things of the new Earth which are largely spiritual. They miss the old ways and still prefer to live in the old ways. When the man arrives to help, they will be rather reticent of his presence and it will take time before they accept him into their community of criminals and thieves. Eventually, the man will convince the followers of Satan to give up their selfish desires for better and more fruitful lives. They will also ask to be allowed back into the nations of new Earth and will be accepted.

In time, all of humanity on new Earth will become friends and will cooperate to make each other's lives even more comfortable. The new Earth will eventually be a paradise as all the people of new Earth cooperate with each other to the fullest. The new Earth will turn into a world full of peace and joy with technology that will rival anything produced by the old Earth. This new technology will turn landscapes into the most beautiful scenery ever seen by human hands. It will cull out the old growth trees and protect them from encroachment and preserve the beauty that exists on new Earth. This same technology will enhance the food crops and vegetable crops and nut crops as well. It will be an eye-opening experience for everyone who witnesses the transformation. The new advanced technology will also be able to enhance the lifespan of everyone on new Earth. Instead of living for less than a hundred years in most cases, they will be able to live for hundreds of years. What will it be like to have thousands of grandchildren, great-grandchildren, great-great grandchildren, and great-great-great grandchildren and know all of their names and all of the names of their children and so on and so on? Just imagine what a family reunion might look like for parents who have lived for hundreds of years. It would be attended by thousands of people, all related and each knowing everyone else. How would you like to prepare a meal for all of those people? A catering service would have to have hundreds of people just to attend to everyone's needs. This should give us an idea of what the new Earth will one day be like after all evil influences from Satan has been removed for all time.

We Can Speak to the Animals

Still, there is more our Lord Christ Jesus explained to me concerning the new Earth you may not know. For instance, the new Earth will be populated with all kinds of plants, animals, fish, and birds. But, there will be no insects, arachnids, or snakes. It will be like a paradise and there will be no wild animals that consume another animal or prey on people in order to survive. Only large herbivores will live on new Earth including fish and birds. There will be all kinds of beautiful birds with beautiful plumage and even the fish will be very beautiful. The herbivores will be beautiful as well. Everything will look more vivid in color than we now see on Earth. This is because the new Earth will be more spiritual in nature and less physical in nature. This will help all life live longer and have virtually no pain or discomfort. Although, there will be instances that pain could bring discomfort to an animal or even a human. Perhaps by an accident or unintended injury. Still, by and large, most life on new Earth will be pain free and live long and healthy lives. Also, the wild animals will not be aggressive toward humans and in some instances, we will be able to speak with them and they will understand what we are saying. We can have a conversation with a Giraffe if we want and find out what kind of food they enjoy eating. A Lion may wander by and stop to speak with us. Yes, there will be Lions and Tigers; however, they will be very docile and will not attack other animals to eat them. You will be able to approach them and pet them. They will eat mostly some fish and fruits and berries and even some will eat grass of various varieties. I know this sounds strange, but it is something we may see in the future if we should find ourselves on the new Earth.

If you happen to find yourself there on new Earth you may be happy to know you will not have to eat three meals a day. You may eat small meals of fruit, seeds, berries, some fish, and nuts. However, our Lord God will be very unhappy with us if we should kill an animal to eat. This act would make us a prey animal and frighten all of the other docile animals. Some may eat the flesh of animals; however, very few people of new Earth will eat the flesh of anything except fish. We will need little food since we are more spiritual in being and less physical. What this means is, we will be able to absorb some of our food from the surrounding atmosphere and therefore we will need less physical food than we needed on old Earth. We will all look physically fit and very athletic and a very handsome race of people. Child birth will be pain free and we will all have large families since we will not have to work for our food. It will be in plentiful supply. The new Earth will be far larger than old Earth and, in the beginning, there will be few people actually populating new Earth. In time, as the population grows we will begin to create structures to live in instead of living in crude shelters. Team work will play a big part in forming shelters and small villages. As mentioned earlier, eventually we will have a worldwide civilization that works in cooperation to construct impressive structures, roads, and highways. We will be environmentally friendly and have no forms of energy that require destroying forests to build large power plants. In fact, we will all be energy independent and have abundant energy for all. It will be free energy. To have to pay for energy will be considered an abomination. Energy should be freely available to everyone. The energy we will have will not pollute our environment. The influence of our Lord God in our lives will guide our technological development. In addition, there will be no need for jails, prisons, sanitoriums, mental institutions. Such institutions will have no place on new Earth.

Now, getting back to Revelation chapter 23. It appears there is still some evil in new Earth as revealed in Revelation 21:17 and Revelation 22:15.

Revelation 21:27

"Nothing evil will be allowed to enter, nor anyone who practices shameful idolatry and dishonesty--but only those whose names are written in the Lamb's Book of Life."

Revelation 22:15

"Outside the city are the dogs--the sorcerers, the sexually immoral, the murderers, the idol worshipers, and all who love to live a lie."

Even in new Earth there will still be people such as these. What we find in chapter 21 is a bit of a quandary. How is it that our Lord God will be living amongst us and yet there will still be people who are worshiping false gods and still practicing sorcery and adulterers? At this point I would like offer a solution to this quandary. For instance, many have believed we live more than one life. If we lived but one lifetime then all of the millions of people alive on Earth when our Lord Christ Jesus walked this Earth and who never heard or laid eyes on our Lord Christ Jesus would have gone to hell. This situation would demonstrate that our Lord God had not planned well in order to save as many people on Earth as possible, if it were true. However, our Lord God did plan well indeed and just below you will read holy Scripture confirming that fact. Let us begin with Matthew.

Matthew 16:13-14
"When Jesus came to the region of Caesarea Philippi, he asked his disciples, 'Who do people say that the Son of Man is?'

"Well," they replied, "some say John the Baptist, some say Elijah, and others say Jeremiah or one of the other prophets"(NLT).

Matthew 17:10-13
"Then his disciples asked him, 'Why do the teachers of religious law insist that Elijah must return before the Messiah comes?'

"Jesus replied, 'Elijah is indeed coming first to get everything ready. But I tell you, Elijah has already come, but he wasn't recognized, and they chose to abuse him. And in the same way they will also make the Son of Man suffer.' Then the disciples realized he was talking about John the Baptist"(NLT).

The next quote is taken from my book *In the Beginning.* "In Luke 1:15-17, the angel Gabriel explains to Zechariah that he and his wife Elizabeth would give birth to a child, and he is to be named John. '...He will be filled with the Holy Spirit even before his birth. And he will turn many Israelites to the Lord their God. He will be a man with the spirit and power of Elijah'" (*In the Beginning*, 2022, 3rd Edition).

John the Baptist will be filled with the spirit and power of Elijah. And, he will prepare the way for the coming Messiah, our Lord Christ Jesus. Our Lord Christ Jesus told his disciples to spread the Word to all the Earth, which did not happen during his lifetime; but, only in the known world at that time. The people living in the Middle East did not know of the millions of people living in the America's. This begs the question; Would our Lord God allow millions of people worldwide to go to hell without ever hearing the Good News? It would be exceedingly unfair and cruel if our Lord God were to let millions of His own children burn in hell for all eternity and this is apparently what many believe must have happened. I should clarify that eternity is a period of a thousand years and does not mean forever. We may burn in hell for a thousand years and then we will be freed from hell and then journey to hades to recuperate before once again returning to Earth to inhabit a new body to live another lifetime. Below is yet another verse where Christ Jesus speaks of John the Baptist as being Elijah. Christ Jesus states that John the Baptist is Elijah reborn in the holy Scripture.

Matthew 11:11-15

"I tell you the truth, of all who have ever lived, none is greater than John the Baptist. Yet even the least person in the Kingdom of Heaven is greater than he is! And from the time John the Baptist began preaching until now, the Kingdom of Heaven has been forcefully advancing, and violent people are attacking it. For before John came, all the prophets and the law of Moses looked forward to this present time. And if you are willing to accept what I say, he is Elijah, the one the prophets said would come. Anyone with ears to hear should listen and understand!"(NLT).

The above verse says it very plainly. John the Baptist is Elijah reborn.

Returning to the situation of the world at that time and the present time where millions on Earth did not know of our Lord Christ Jesus, there is another explanation which actually fits much better and would not allow millions of people to burn in hell for all eternity because they were born in the wrong place at the wrong time. Here is that explanation, and it is not anything new, it is a belief thousands of years old and that is, we live many lifetimes. The old saying that you only live once is wrong. We are spiritual beings living in an earthly body and that earthly body will eventually reach its useful ends. However, as spiritual beings we can never die. When our bodies die we are still live on in spirit. Our bodies are buried with our family and friends present.

So, where do we go once we die? We may go to heaven if we are true Christians; however, if we are not we may go to hell by Satan's decree. But, there is another place to go for those who do not go to heaven or hell and that place is called Hades or Purgatory. "The Hebrew word "*sheol*" is translated as "*hades*" in Greek and "*purgatorio*" in Latin." (Source:Catholic.net) There are conflicting accounts of whether hades or purgatory is a place of punishment or a paradise. I was told by our Lord Christ Jesus that hades is a place of rest and recuperation for all Souls who come there before returning to Earth to be reborn once again, usually, to someone they knew on Earth and most likely knew through many lifetimes. Hades is far out in the heavens and is a spiritual abode. In hades we can recuperate from being in hell for a period of time before we are once again reborn into a human body in order to try once more to find our Lord Christ Jesus and accept him as our Lord and Savior. Others are there due to not being a good enough Christian to make it to heaven. They too will rest and recuperate from an often-abusive life which may be the result of war as a soldier or a civilian who may have suffered greatly during their lifetime. And for others, it may be they never accepted our Lord Christ Jesus as their Savior and still lived a relatively giving life. Perhaps as a caretaker, a doctor, a mother with many children to care for. People like these and others such as police and firefighters who put their lives on the line to help and save others. Others were like most people who live their lives without receiving much in the way of spiritual training. Perhaps they were never exposed to a Church environment or attended Church at all. The belief in our Lord Christ Jesus as a Savior was all nonsense to them and they chose to believe there was no God and certainly no Satan. So, they ended up in hades to return one day again to Earth and hopefully, eventually, find our Lord Christ Jesus and accept him as Lord and Savior and then make it to heaven. Our Lord Christ has returned many times according to what Christ Jesus said to me, to sacrifice himself over and over again for all humanity over the millions of years humans have lived on Earth. Each time he comes our Lord Christ saves many Souls and returns them to heaven.

Keep in mind that no matter if we go to hell or hades, one day we will again be given the opportunity to be reborn on Earth until we finally accept our Lord Christ Jesus as our Lord and Savior, who will forgive us of our many sins. Without forgiveness of our many sins accumulated over many thousands of lifetimes, we cannot return to heaven. Our sins stain our Soul and we have a spiritual stench about us. Unless we receive forgiveness of our sins our Lord God will not allow us in heaven where our stench would set us apart. Sin is from the evil one and as long as our Soul is stained with sin we are still connected to Satan. Our sins make us unclean.

To end on a happy note, one day we will have all returned to our Father in heaven where all is pure and beautiful, where angels soar all around us and peace reigns and beautiful music can be heard from our Lord God who is the greatest composer of all. Where all of the people we have once loved and all the children we have had over many lifetimes on Earth will be with us and so will our Lord Christ Jesus and The Holy Spirit and our Lord God. It will be as it was intended. We will love everyone and everyone will love us. There will be no more pain or suffering. No more tears and no more sorrows. Only joy and peace.

So, ends "Revelation Revealed: A Modern Interpretation." We do hope you enjoyed our version of the Book of Revelation. There has been so much written on the Book of Revelation since it was first read by the Churches in Asia Minor it could literally make volumes of books if it were all written down. Here, in this book lies one more work to add to that volume of many works concerning the prophecy's written of in the Book of Revelation.

CHAPTER 23

Speaking with The Holy Spirit

This final chapter is for all of those who have never given much attention to The Holy Spirit. Our Lord Christ Jesus made The Holy Spirit a special gift to each of his followers, yet, most of us hardly know that The Holy Spirit even exists. Our Lord God, our Lord Christ Jesus, and The Holy Spirit have a pure love untainted by selfish needs.

During my encounter with Satan and his demons, which I wrote about in my first book called "Satan's World" I wrote quite a bit concerning The Holy Spirit. I actually prayed for almost three days battling Satan and his demons before I heard a very friendly voice that brought me great comfort. It was the most wonderful and the sweetest voice I have ever heard. It immediately got my attention and I very shyly asked who it was. The Holy Spirit responded with, "This is your Holy Spirit." I replied with, "What do you mean by, "my Holy Spirit." This is when The Holy Spirit explained why he introduced himself as my Holy Spirit. The Holy Spirit reminded me that our Lord Christ Jesus had given The Holy Spirit to me as a gift. This is when I realized I had forgot all about that. I had not remembered The Holy Spirit dwells within me and within you as well, if you are a follower of our Lord Christ Jesus. At that moment I felt at peace and calm. It was the most peacefully feeling I had ever felt. I had some trepidation that The Holy Spirit would chastise me for the sinful things I had done. However, I was very wrong. The Holy Spirit was so polite and so concerned with the situation I was going through and he never once chastised me for even the slightest sin. The Holy Spirit turned out to be more polite and more courteous than anyone I have ever known.

During my ordeal with Satan and his demons The Holy Spirit gave me encouragement and a prayer that would help me defeat Satan and his demons. It was a prayer that actually caused Satan and his demons' great pain and would eventually drive then away, but in the beginning only for a relatively short time. After driving Satan or one of his demons away, I could then relax and recoup my strength and rest to continue my fight for my Soul. I still speak with The Holy Spirit to this day. Notice how I type 'The Holy Spirit.' I do this to emphasize there is only one Holy Spirit and due to the fact that The Holy Spirit prefers it that way. I actually spoke with our Lord Christ Jesus as well. This happened the first time five days after first hearing the demonic voice of Satan telling me that I would "Bleep my bleeping brains out before the night was over." When I heard Satan's evil sounding voice I knew I was in deep trouble. I immediately dropped to my knees on the floor and began praying with all my Soul. I did not know who to pray to so I began praying to both our Lord God and our Lord Christ Jesus. I prayed for hours each day in order to drive away Satan or his demon. Sometimes a demon would torment me and Satan would be off somewhere else. I prayed this way until The Holy Spirit gave me what is called a blood prayer where you invoke the 'Blood of Christ' to protect yourself and possessions from evil. This is why I feel I am qualified to write this chapter on how to properly address The Holy Spirit. So, I hope you will enjoy this rather short chapter. Hopefully, it might someday come in handy for your needs. Now, without further ado, how to properly address and speak to The Holy Spirit.

Speaking to The Holy Spirit

First of all, I want to tell all of my readers something they should know concerning The Holy Spirit, and that is, when you speak to The Holy Spirit, always speak in a very low whisper or speak to The Holy Spirit in your mind. Also, always address The Holy Spirit with a leading "The" since there is only one Holy Spirit. After you initially address The Holy Spirit you can then address him further as Holy Spirit for some short time. Then, after some short time has passed you should address The Holy Spirit with the leading "The" once again. The time frame for when to address The Holy Spirit with a leading 'The' varies; however, I would not wait too long. The Holy Spirit likes for us to remember who we are speaking with. It is a reminder for us and a show of respect for The Holy Spirit.

Now, getting back to my first point concerning addressing The Holy Spirit. I am sure we are all familiar with thinking in our minds, where we think out ways to solve problems and think them through silently in our minds, looking at every conceivable way we might make a mistake if we should decide to make one decision verses another decision. We look at all the different possibilities that might interfere with our decision and adjust accordingly until we are satisfied this time we have it all thought through. So, we all speak to ourselves in our mind from time to time to test out an idea to think it through and see if it will work.

Let me give you a rather long explanation of speaking in our minds versus speaking out loud, which we never want to do with The Holy Spirit. If we speak out loud to The Holy Spirit is hurts his feelings very much. One reason The Holy Spirit is named The Holy Spirit is due to the highly sensitive nature of The Holy Spirit.

If we would rather speak out loud to The Holy Spirit we must speak in a very low whisper. Do not forget that although The Holy Spirit will more than likely forgive us should we speak to loudly and hurt his feelings, we should try our best to not hurt his feelings.

Now, getting back to that lengthy explanation of what it is like to speak within our minds. It does take some practice to speak with The Holy Spirit in our minds only.

A Short Example to Follow

For instance, here is an exchange between a car salesman and a potential car buyer.

A young woman rehearsing to speak with a car dealer about purchasing a new bright green car. She is speaking to herself in her mind. Small quotes are used with the car buyer and car dealer when speaking to themselves in their mind.

Car Buyer: 'I want to buy this car with cash and I want it with a pink interior, at no additional charge. Can you make that happen for me?'

Then the car buyer might ask herself this question internally.

Car Buyer: 'What might he think by the way I stated that question?'

Then perhaps she speaks to a friend about her idea and asks them what they might think the car dealer might say about it.

Car Buyer's Friend: "I do not know. Maybe he will look at you funny and smile, and then might say, "You want a pink interior? Is that what you are asking for?" "

Then your friend might look at you and ask;

Car Buyer's Friend: "Why do you want a pink interior when the exterior is green?"

Then the car buyer in her mind she thinks;

Car Buyer: 'That is an absurd question, is it not?'

Anyway, she sticks to her guns and walks down to the dealership to find that beautiful green car she wants and speaks with the car dealer and asks him that same question she spoke about concerning the pink interior to herself. The salesman looks at her and says;

Car Dealer: "If that is what you want I will see what I can do."

Then he walks off and her hopes sky rocket believing that she might get her wish. Then, after a while the car dealer returns and tells her;

Car Dealer: "No, I am sorry. It does not come in a pink interior, unless you change the exterior color."

Then the car buyer might respond with;

Car Buyer: "Why would I have to do that for?"

The salesman explains;

Car Dealer: "Because green does not go with pink."

Then the girl responded with;

Car Buyer: "That is my decision, is it not?"

The salesman then says;

Car Dealer: "Not really, since you might change your mind on buying the car once you see the stark color contrast. What would we do with a car that nobody wants."

Then the girl responds with;

Car Buyer: "I promise you, I will not change my mind, okay? I will give that to you in writing."

The salesman replies;

Car Dealer: "I am sorry, but my showroom boss says, 'No can do.'"

The young lady, visibly upset that she cannot have the car of her dreams, then walks away with a dejected look on her face.

Car Buyer: 'What will I do now?'

She asks herself once again in her mind.

This is the end of my lengthy explanation. But, I am sure you get the point. Sometimes we speak aloud and sometimes we speak to ourselves in our mind. The only difference is that when speaking with The Holy Spirit we must speak in our mind or with a very quiet whisper that no one else in the room can hear.

Do try to speak with The Holy Spirit because he loves you so very much. More so than we can possibly imagine and The Holy Spirit misses us so much. I got rather emotional when The Holy Spirit first expressed how much he had missed me. You see, we were all created in heaven from almost the beginning of our Lord God's creation of all things. We are Spirit as our Father in heaven is Spirit. We never actually die.

I asked The Holy Spirit how he could miss me so much and The Holy Spirit replied that he has known me and loved me since my creation and it has been so very long since we had last spoke to one another. Ever since I was last born on Earth several lifetimes ago. The Holy Spirit loves you that much as well so speak with The Holy Spirit and in due time The Holy Spirit with speak to you. And, you will know it is The Holy Spirit from his nonjudgmental voice. The Holy Spirit may become your best friend.

So ends our modern interpretation of the Book of Revelation. We do hope you are less frightened of what the near future might bring your way. Adios for now my friends.

THE END